AN

S

BUT

HAPPY

NIC LUCAS

Author of *Possibility to Actuality*

Anxious but Happy

Nicholas Lucas
BSc, MHSc, MPainMed, GDipClinEpid

Research Media, Sydney, Australia, 2009
808/109 Pitt St, Sydney NSW 2000, Australia

Published by Research Media

ISBN: 1439265879
ISBN-13: 9781439265871
Library of Congress Control Number: 2009911595

The procedures and practices described in this book should be implemented in a manner consistent with professional standards set for the circumstances that apply in each situation. Every effort has been made to confirm accuracy of the information presented and correctly relate generally accepted practices.

The author and publisher cannot accept responsibility for errors or exclusions or for the outcome of the application of the material presented herein. There is no expressed or implied warranty of this book or information imparted by it.

Research Media
808/109 Pitt St, Sydney
NSW 2000 Australia
+61 2 9233 2788

www.fromanxioustohappy.com
www.niclucas.com

Lucas, Nicholas
Anxious but Happy
First published 2009

ISBN: 978-0-9806192-0-1

National Library of Australia
A catalogue record for this book is available from the National Library of Australia

State Library of NSW
A catalogue record of this book is available from the State Library of NSW

Dedication and Acknowledgements

It is with gratitude that I dedicate this book to Rhoda Lucas. Not only was she my guardian angel during the years of my anxiety, but she has continued to be completely supportive throughout the planning, research and writing of this book. Rhoda has made this massive task so much easier.

Thanks to everyone else who has been supportive of me – specifically in relation to this project. Thanks to those friends and colleagues who didn't get 'weirded out' when I announced that I had anxiety – this was the best thing you could have done. I only hope others are so fortunate. Thanks to Rob and all the Peters. A special thanks to Brett who not only encouraged me to write this book, but showed me how and held me accountable in terms of finishing it. So, hey presto, here it is.

Lastly, thanks to my kids, Harley and Lara. They don't really know it yet, but they contribute significant inspiration.

But first, some important and serious stuff...

The information in this book can help you understand the diagnosis and treatment of anxiety disorders, but is not intended to be a substitute for individual medical diagnosis. You are advised to consult with your personal healthcare professional for accurate diagnosis and treatment before applying any of the information contained in this book.

The symptoms of panic attacks and anxiety can occur as a result of another medical condition or as a symptom of other medication or recreational drug use. All reference to panic attacks and anxiety in this book are related to those for which there is no other medical or substance cause.

The major focus of the book is on panic disorder and generalised anxiety disorder. The author does include information about phobias, social anxiety, obsessive-compulsive disorder and posttraumatic stress disorder; however the author does not have personal experience of these anxiety disorders.

Navigation

Foreword

Anxiety Disorders are some of the most common clinical mental health diagnoses with too many sufferers remaining undiagnosed and untreated. Everyone experiences anxiety at certain times, as this is a normal reaction to stress. It accompanies tense situations e.g. prior to exams and public speaking and helps one remain focused on that task. However, when anxiety becomes an excessive and irrational dread of everyday situations it can become a disabling disorder that may become worse over time.

Many therapies exist for anxiety disorders and research is informing health professionals and the public about which treatments might be most effective in helping sufferers with anxiety disorders lead productive and fulfilling lives.

Nic Lucas has produced a highly informative book that deals with anxiety as viewed through the prism of his own experiences and written in a light hearted manner that belies to some extent the degree to which sufferers of anxiety disorders can be disabled by their condition. A reassuring message is that anxiety disorder is common and you are not alone. There are strategies for managing and overcoming the, sometimes crippling, effects of excessive and uncontrollable anxiety.

The author takes us through an explanation of the different classifications of anxiety disorder including panic disorder, generalised anxiety disorder, agoraphobia, social phobia, specific phobia (or social anxiety disorder), obsessive compulsive disorder and post-traumatic stress disorder, in a language that the lay reader can understand. Each anxiety disorder has different symptoms, but all the symptoms cluster around excessive and irrational fear.

It is likely that readers will recognise certain presentations that remind them of their own experiences or those of relatives or friends. This is a book for sufferers of anxiety or for those who want to better understand and possibly support friends or relatives with an anxiety disorder.

Nic also describes the symptoms of anxiety disorders and, using simple analogies from everyday life, helps the reader understand potential causes of these conditions, outlines both pharmacologic and non-pharmacologic treatments and provides an overview of the current research that supports or refutes certain clinical interventions.

The development of physical dependency when using pharmacologic treatments often worries both clinicians and patients, but are there meaningful alternatives to drug treatment? Nic presents a research-based overview in a manner that is easy to understand and does not confound the reader with unintelligible medical jargon.

Those of you who read this book because you believe that you may have an anxiety disorder are fortunate. An overwhelming number of people with anxiety disorders remain undiagnosed and untreated. The author presents essential information for sufferers of anxiety disorders in an easy to read format. Readers of this book will be able to recognise the features of the different anxiety disorders and have access to essential information regarding treatment options based upon current research findings.

It is essential that sufferers of anxiety disorder are better informed about their condition as, in today's health care environment, their treating physician may not have the time or even knowledge to provide optimal care. This book provides an essential overview of anxiety disorder written in manner that lay people can understand and provides essential information for sufferers wanting to take some control of their own symptoms and treatment.

It is my opinion that this book fills a need for a well written dissertation on the subject of anxiety disorders clearly directed at the sufferer or their relatives and friends who would like to better understand the condition. It is clear, concise, accurate, easily readable and recommended.

Dr Peter Gibbons
MB BS, DO, DM-SMed, MHSc
Melbourne, Victoria
Australia

Preface: Why I wrote this book and how it can help you

I wrote this book about anxiety to discuss how I managed it and how I got over it. If you read it, it may just help you manage and get over it – so that you can get on with it.

This is the book I wish I'd had when I had anxiety disorder.

I wrote this book to heroically laugh in the face of anxiety. Sometimes I don't think that there's much to laugh about when it comes to anxiety and panic disorder…but thankfully 'humour', 'anxiety' and 'panic' are produced by different parts of the brain, and humour can sometimes win.

I'm living proof that you can be ***anxious but happy,*** which is how I describe the final two years of my recovery from anxiety and panic disorder. During this time, I wasn't sure that I'd ever completely recover from anxiety. I'd learnt how to deal with anxiety and I was living a happy and successful life despite my excessive feelings of anxiety. So, this is why this book earned the title, *Anxious but Happy.*

I'm also living proof that you can be happy and ***not*** anxious. I completely overcame anxiety disorder, and at the time of writing, I haven't experienced any abnormal anxiety or panic attacks in the last seven years. After writing this book, I decided to document the techniques and strategies that I discovered and used during my recovery. I have written a companion to this book called, *From Anxious to Happy: A manual for overcoming anxiety and panic attacks.*

This manual is available at www.fromanxioustohappy.com

"The purpose of life is to live it, to taste experience to the utmost, to reach out eagerly and without fear for newer and richer experience"

This is how Eleanor Roosevelt described it. And you can't really live life like this if you're anxious or having random panic attacks that leave you unable to enjoy or even participate in life.

Who knows, you might be feeling anxious right now, just because you're reading this book. Reading about anxiety used to make me feel anxious too. So, put down the book if you need to. I'm not going anywhere...I can wait. You'll come back when you're ready.

But if you're ready now, then get stuck into this book.

I start by briefly describing the various types of anxiety disorder, and you may recognise that you fall into one definite category. Of course, self-diagnosis is always a bit dodgy, and I recommend you consult with a qualified and interested health care professions; however, you may be someone who will never consult a psychiatrist or psychologist for your anxiety, and so you can use the first chapter in this book to get a general idea of where you fit into the spectrum of anxiety disorders.

I then take a brief look at the evidence for *who* gets anxiety disorder. This is a useful read, if only it let's you know that you're not alone, and than anxiety disorder is common.

Once you know a bit more about anxiety and panic attacks, I tell my story. I didn't have a burning desire to publicise my history of anxiety to the world – but in my work as a health professional, I have found that by sharing my story with patients, I have been able to help them take the first real steps toward overcoming anxiety.

I am not a psychiatrist, psychologist or trained counsellor – I work with people in physical pain – but a lot of the people I see are also anxious and have panic attacks; so it comes up a lot in my work.

Often I'm the first health professional – and sometimes the first person – they have ever told about their anxiety problem; and that is why I decided to write this book, so that I could leverage my time and knowledge and increase the number of people I may be able to help.

After telling my story, I then take you through some background information on 'how' anxiety happens. I don't go into massive details here, and I use the Internet as an analogy for our brain. By understanding how anxiety and panic attacks work, you have a better chance at changing and controlling the experience.

The main thing on people's minds, however, is treatment; how can they make it go away? What can they do? What can they take? For this I discuss the evidence for the majority of different treatment options available. I did my best to keep this section light hearted and tried not to regurgitate boring textbook and research material; but I have drawn heavily on the most recent evidence in order to equip you with the most useful knowledge.

After the exposé on treatments for anxiety and panic attacks, I come to a close in a brief summary chapter – a left over chapter where I squeezed in a few other ideas and information that didn't have a place elsewhere in the book.

I have a kept the book as brief as I can and used analogies and stories to explain the major concepts. Anxiety and panic attacks are hard enough without having to wade through boring or overly detailed writing.

I look forward to receiving your feedback – good or bad. In fact, constructive criticism is encouraged because I want this book to be as good as it can be. You can email me directly at info@niclucas.com.

Wishing you all the best,

Nic Lucas

1

Anxiety: such an inadequate word to describe the experience

Anyone reading this book who has had daily anxiety or panic attacks will appreciate the title of this chapter. Anxiety: such a little word that is supposed to sum up such an enormous experience. Anyone reading this book that has *not* had anxiety or panic attacks will find it difficult to imagine just how severe anxiety and panic attacks can be.

Perhaps that's why you're reading this book – to find out more so that you can understand a friend, lover, colleague, or family member.

Why is anxiety an inadequate word?

I think that the word 'anxiety' is an inadequate word to describe anxiety disorder and panic attacks because everyone, at some time, experiences 'anxiety', and it can be passed off as something minor, something easy to deal with, something understandable. In fact, when it comes to anxiety disorder and panic attacks, these are anything but minor, easy to deal with, or understandable.

So, first, let's deal with normal everyday 'anxiety'; what I call 'worry' or being 'stressed' or 'nervous'.

Being worried about something is being focussed on the potential of an unpleasant experience or outcome.

Being late. Failing an exam. Having an interview. Being in a sport final. Just about to participate in an Olympic event (common to most of us!). Meeting your partner's parents for the first time. Missing your mortgage repayment. Being chased by a dog; and for some, having a bad hair day.

These are all normal things to be 'worried' about. Feeling worried is having a slight sinking feeling, or tightening, in your stomach or chest. You might feel your heart rate go up. You might feel the need to take a deep breath.

We've all been 'worried'.

This isn't anxiety disorder and it definitely isn't a panic attack. The anxiety that people with *anxiety disorder* experience is excessive. It is inappropriate. It is a complete over reaction in comparison to the *stimulus* or situation. People with anxiety disorder aren't delusional, so they know that the reaction is excessive. Knowing this doesn't make any difference to someone with anxiety disorder. In fact, knowing that the anxiety response is excessive is a real source of additional worry.

Pointing out to someone with anxiety disorder that they are over reacting will probably be met with a derogatory "no kidding" response from them; it might not a good idea to point out the obvious...

Officially anxious?

According to the American Psychiatric Association,[1] anxiety disorder is the official name for a whole range of different anxiety experiences. Anxiety disorder includes panic disorder, generalised anxiety disorder, agoraphobia, social phobia, specific phobia, obsessive compulsive disorder (OCD), and post traumatic stress disorder.

And it's important to get the terminology correct.

The reason for all the different names is because people experience anxiety and panic attacks *differently*, and the names help to identify these differences. It is important to identify these differences because the causes, treatment and prognosis for the *different* types can be, surprisingly, *different*.

Example

Let me give you an example. People with OCD have unreasonable and recurrent obsessions or compulsions that take up a whole lot of time and cause severe distress. For example, they may become anxious and panic over whether or not they washed their hands, with their main problem being recurrent and intruding thoughts about cleanliness and hygiene.

In order to avoid these anxious feelings, people with OCD will compulsively wash their hands to make sure that they are clean – really clean. Washing their hands *relieves* their anxiety about cleanliness and hygiene – and if they are unable to wash their hands they will experience anxiety, and they may panic.

People who have social anxiety disorder become anxious and panic about public speaking, but have no obsessive or recurrent thoughts – they only become anxious if they have to speak publicly. Clearly these two people are quite different, even though they both experience anxiety and panic as common symptoms.

It's important to recognise that these *anxiety disorder* labels are based on established criteria that have been agreed upon by a group of people fondly referred to as medical experts – they are not based on a diagnostic test, even though the psychiatrists and psychologists call them *diagnoses.*

With so many different types of anxiety labels or *diagnoses* for anxiety disorder, you can imagine that sometimes there is some overlap – and even the experts can have difficulty saying which label is the correct one.

All of the very detailed criteria for each of the anxiety disorders are published by the American Psychiatric Association in the Diagnostic and Statistical Manual of Mental Disorders (DSM)

And guess what...people are allowed to have more than one problem or label, but in keeping with the style of this book, I'm going to describe these all fairly simply and using plain language.

For the formal academic definition, go my website: www.fromanxioustohappy.com/definitions.html

An introduction to each of the anxiety 'disorders'

Let's start with panic attacks. When a person has a panic attack, they experience intense fear. This fear comes on fast and peaks within about 10 – 20 minutes.

Panic attacks can occur with or without agoraphobia (a fear of open spaces) and have any four of the following kinds of 'lovely' symptoms: heart palpitations, pounding heart, or accelerated heart rate, sweating, trembling or shaking, sensations of shortness of breath or a smothering feeling, choking, chest pain or discomfort, nausea or abdominal distress, feeling dizzy, unsteady, lightheaded, or faint, feelings of unreality or of being detached from oneself, fear of losing control or of going crazy, fear of dying, numbness or tingling sensations, and chills or hot flushes.

Funny how some of those feelings (pounding heart, trembling) could also be associated with pleasure or excitement – damn we're complicated.

Panic attacks can occur in different types of anxiety disorder – but can also occur in non-psychological medical conditions. For this reason, people don't get diagnosed with 'panic attacks'. Instead, panic attacks are considered to be a symptom of an underlying disorder.

So what's the story with Panic Disorder?

When someone has experienced at least two unexpected panic attacks over a period of a month, they are said to have Panic Disorder, and unlike panic attacks, Panic Disorder *is* an official diagnosis. People will usually have many more than two unexpected attacks, however, just because you've had one panic attack doesn't mean that you will have more.

Some information on the Internet suggests that there is also another disorder called 'anxiety attacks'. An 'anxiety attack', however, isn't recognised in the Diagnostic and Statistical Manual of Mental Disorders. It's important to use the 'accepted' labels as this helps to avoid confusion and probably helps to reduce anxiety!

People can also have what are called *cued* or *situational* panic attacks – because they are always triggered by an identifiable 'cue' or 'situation'. That cue may be external, like a place, animal or object; or it may be internal, like a thought or a physical sensation, such as heart palpitations or nausea.

In addition, people become understandably worried about the panic attacks they are having, and so they experience what is called 'anticipatory anxiety' in-between each of the panic attacks.

A bit about me

I had panic disorder – although over time I came to understand what was triggering the panic attacks, and therefore the attacks stopped being *unexpected* and became *situational* or *cued.* Of course, I continued to be anxious in-between each panic attack, and so also had anticipatory anxiety. Then, after I learned how to stop having panic attacks I continued to experience daily anxiety, and so then had what they call Generalised Anxiety Disorder. Nice one...

Generalised Anxiety Disorder (GAD)

Generalised anxiety disorder (GAD) is when you wake up virtually every day and feel excessively anxious – and you can't shut it off. You might get a couple of seconds when you wake up and feel 'normal', but as soon as you become self-aware, that 'worried' feeling fills you up. The anxiety is more intense than 'normal' anxiety, and on top of this you may have absolutely no idea *why* you are feeling this way. You feel restless and on edge. It's hard to concentrate and you often feel tired and irritable. And this lasts all day.

The intensity of the experience may fluctuate, and at times during they day a person with GAD may not be aware of anxious feelings; GAD, however, is persistent.

Wake with it. Live with it. Go to sleep with it.

But wait...there's more. Quite a lot of people with GAD and Panic Disorder can also experience the unusual feelings of *depersonalisation* and *derealisation*. These aren't typical everyday experiences associated with 'normal worry'. They're definitely strange, weird and disconcerting feelings.

Depersonalisation is when you feel a sense of unreality and detachment from yourself. You feel disconnected from your body as if you are observing yourself. You feel like it's all a bit of a dream.

You might be talking to someone and feeling highly anxious – but the person you're talking to doesn't know this. So, you have these bizarre mental acrobatics going on in your head where you're listening to what they're saying – or what you're saying – but at the same time you're feeling highly anxious – watching yourself from a distance.

People who have depersonalisation often experience **derealisation** as well. The external environment appears unfamiliar, other people appear as though they are actors, and the world appears two-dimensional.

Now, if you were feeling anxious for no apparent reason, and if the anxiety you were feeling was far more intense than what you would consider to be 'normal', would that make you concerned? I mean, if there was nothing else the matter, wouldn't that potentially make you feel anxious? And if all of a sudden the world seemed strange, you felt disconnected from your body and felt like you were in a bit of a dream-state, or you were experiencing any of the additional symptoms of anxiety, wouldn't that also make you feel anxious?

Well, it made me feel anxious. And the problem is summed up in this simple equation:

***Abnormal anxiety* PLUS *other weird feelings* PLUS *a normal anxiety response to the abnormal anxiety and weird feelings* EQUALS a whole lot of anxiety.**

Phobias

Now, on top of all this, many people have *phobias*, and the phobia may actually be the main trigger for panic attacks. A phobia is anything that makes you excessively or unreasonably scared. It could be a specific external trigger, like a spider, or it could be an internal trigger, like a thought or feeling. It could also be a phobia of social situations or public speaking, the so-called social anxiety disorder.

Encountering the trigger usually provokes an immediate anxiety response, which may be a panic attack. The person knows that the fear is excessive or unreasonable, and they will try to avoid the trigger. If they can't avoid it, they literally *endure* the experience in severe distress.

So, someone may only panic when they encounter the object of their phobia. Or, they may start out with a phobia, which develops into panic attacks whenever they encounter their phobia, which may then develop into anticipatory anxiety between each panic attack; oh…and then they may develop generalised anxiety disorder.

And just when you thought that was enough, some people become depressed as well!

I was fortunate enough not to experience depression, and so I feel unqualified to write anything much about it. Suffice to say that the question of whether anxiety and depression are actually along the same continuum is still being debated today. It seems that anxiety and depression frequently overlap and distinguishing between the two disorders can be difficult. This is complicated by the fact that some of the drugs that reduce depression also reduce anxiety.

Obsessive Compulsive Disorder

I briefly mentioned obsessive-compulsive disorder (OCD) above, however I'll describe it in a little more detail. The 'obsessive' parts of OCD are recurrent thoughts, persistent thoughts, and intrusive and inappropriate thoughts that cause severe anxiety or distress. People may also have disturbing visual images pop into their minds in addition to their thoughts.

In response to these obsessions, the person is compelled to perform repetitive behaviours that are related to the obsessions, such as hand washing or checking the door locks, or they may perform repetitive mental acts such as praying or silently repeating words.

They perform these repetitive behaviours or mental acts in order to either prevent something dreadful from happening, or to reduce their distress. The problem is, however, that these behaviours or mental acts are often excessive and interfere with everyday life. They can interfere with work, study, relationships, and intimacy, and they do not realistically neutralise or prevent the dreaded situation.

At some point the person recognizes that their obsessions and compulsions are unreasonable and will try and find some help – or they may just battle on by themselves, without help.

You probably know someone who is 'a bit obsessive'. You may live with a 'clean freak' or a perfectionist. The difference with OCD is that the extent of cleanliness or pedantry is excessive and unreasonable – and interferes with everyday life. It pervades day to day life; and this is what makes it different from 'everyday' obsessions. Its pervasiveness. Its relentlessness.

Pervasiveness - Relentlessness

If you've seen the 1997 film 'As good as it gets' with Jack Nicholson playing the obsessive-compulsive character, then you'll understand what I'm talking about.

Post-Traumatic Stress Disorder

The last anxiety disorder I'll mention is post-traumatic stress disorder (PTSD). As the label suggests, people develop anxiety or panic attacks after experiencing a traumatic event. People who have posttraumatic stress disorder have either experienced or witnessed an actual death or a threatened death; or they may have witnessed serious injury to themselves or others.

The person responds to this traumatic event with intense fear, helplessness, or horror. This traumatic event is persistently re-experienced as a recurrent, distressing and vivid memory.

And these memories create anxiety and panic attacks.

The person can feel as if the traumatic event is recurring, and may have hallucinations and flashback episodes. They experience intense psychological distress to internal or external triggers that resemble an aspect of the traumatic event. They do their best to avoid the triggers by trying to control their thoughts and avoiding certain conversation topics, people and places. They can have sleep problems, anger problems, and concentration problems.

It really messes with their lives and their hope for the future. Even though they share the feelings of anxiety and panic attacks with other people who have anxiety disorder, **you can see that people with posttraumatic stress disorder have a reason for their anxiety.**

And this illustrates my point again that people have different reasons for experiencing anxiety and panic – and these different reasons need to be recognised.

These last two versions of anxiety disorder, OCD and PTSD are quite different from Panic Disorder, GAD, and phobic disorders – although there may be overlap. If you're not sure where you fit in the whole scheme of 'anxiety disorder' and not sure which label is right for you, I recommended that you consult with your trusted and interested healthcare professional in order to ensure that you have the correct diagnosis.

Summary

Anxiety Disorder is an umbrella term for a range of different anxiety or panic experiences.

People can have anxiety disorder, but never have a panic attack. People can have panic attacks, but never experience daily anxiety. People can have panic attacks and then spend all the time in-between each panic attack worrying about the next panic attack. People can have phobias as the trigger for their anxiety, or they can have anxiety without knowing *why* they are anxious.

People can have obsessive thoughts that cause compulsive behaviours – both of which are associated with anxiety and panic attacks; and people can develop chronic daily anxiety in response to a traumatic event – the post-traumatic stress syndrome.

If you would like a more algorithmic approach to this information, go to my website to see how each of these diagnostic labels fit together:

www.fromanxioustohappy.com/definitions

I've based the information on my website on the official DSM-IV TR criteria published by the American Psychiatric Association.

After reading the above descriptions, don't you think that each of these 'disorders' is poorly described by the word 'anxiety'? These people don't just have a bit of worry. It's not just 'nerves'. They are not just 'stressed'. And, unlike the advice they've probably received, they *do* worry about the excessive nature of the symptoms and they *should* be taken seriously.

The last thing that should happen is for these people's symptoms to be swept under the proverbial carpet. This only makes matters worse and can drive people into a lonely, long-term and desperate struggle.

Each of these disorders sucks life out of people; causes great distress and fear, and makes day-to-day life difficult. These disorders really are the opposite of hope and the opposite of joy; and they could almost be considered the opposite of *living* life. People with anxiety aren't delusional, and they have *normal* anxiety about the fact that they've got anxiety disorder. **It's a double whammy.**

That's why in this book I talk about taking the anxiety out of anxiety disorder.

By understanding anxiety disorder and by increasing your confidence in managing it, you can become less anxious about having it; and if you can manage that, then the anxiety equation looks like this:

Abnormal anxiety PLUS other weird feelings with LESS of the normal anxiety response to the abnormal anxiety and weird feelings EQUALS not as much anxiety as before,

and this is a great start toward overcoming abnormal anxiety for good.

So, in order to begin to understand anxiety disorder and panic attacks, let's take a look at how common anxiety disorders are and who gets them.

2

Who gets anxiety?

When I first began to have panic attacks and then anxiety, I didn't know anyone else who had the same problem. This was very isolating. Also, as we all know, there's this stigma thing associated with 'mental illness'.

My experience was that people were not shocked to hear that I had anxiety. Mostly they were concerned for me and told me stories of other people they knew who had anxiety. For me, not telling other people had a lot more to do with *me* being fearful of what might happen if I told them; there was also a bit of pride in the way.

Finding out that lots of people have anxiety disorder and panic attacks was actually quite a relief. That's one of the main reasons I've written this book. If you feel 'less anxious' by reading this and understanding that many other people have anxiety, then I will have helped you begin to take the anxiety out of your anxiety disorder. **A small step, but an important step**.

So, who get's anxiety?

The World Health Organisation (WHO) considers anxiety and mood disorders to be amongst the 10 most important public health issues.

They are the most prevalent mental disorders in 13 out of 14 countries surveyed by WHO – so it is fair enough to say that anxiety is wide spread.

In 27 European countries, it was found that of people aged between 18-65, 21% had experienced anxiety at some point in their life, and **12% had experienced an anxiety disorder in the previous 12 months**.

Wow – that's a lot of people. When you really think about it, the footpath, the highways, the cafes and classrooms, etc. are full of people with anxiety disorder.

The American's report that during their lifetime, about 2-4% of people experience panic disorder, 5-7% experience generalised anxiety disorder, 13-16% have social phobia, and another 10% have specific phobia's, while 6% have agoraphobia. 2-3% have obsessive-compulsive disorder and 7-9% have posttraumatic stress disorder.[1]

Oh…and people are allowed to have more than one anxiety disorder at a time. In fact, having one of the anxiety disorders predisposes people to a range of other problems such as depression, alcohol dependence, eating disorders, …the point being that there is a lot of this stuff 'going around'.

Think of a shopping mall – and then think of how many people in that mall have an anxiety disorder; just panic and GAD alone account for about 10 out of every 100 people you see.

Thirty six percent of Australians who were surveyed reported having generalised anxiety disorder in the prior 12 months, and 2.8% in the prior month.[2] That's a lot of anxiety wouldn't you agree? The authors of this survey comment that anxiety is endemic and more research, treatment and education is urgently needed.

People in Pakistan suffer from anxiety disorder. In one particular study, the average prevalence of anxiety and depressive disorders in the community was reported to be 34% (range 29-66% for women and 10-33% for men),[3] which is not dissimilar to other statistics.

People with diabetes get it. A study from the Washington University School of Medicine reports that generalised anxiety disorder is present in 14% of patients with diabetes, and that 40% of patients have elevated symptoms of anxiety.[4]

People with asthma get it. There is an increased chance of anxiety disorder and panic attacks in patients with asthma, as compared to the normal population.[5]

Medical students get it. In a recent review that summarised the findings of 40 separate research articles on medical students in the US and Canada, the Mayo Clinic in the US reports that anxiety and depression are common.[6]

Here's a revelation...**married people get it**. Maria Goldfarb from the University of Quebec reports a strong association between marital dissatisfaction, generalized anxiety disorder and panic disorder.[7]

It also appears that some US Presidents may have suffered from anxiety disorder.[8]

Biographical information regarding the behaviour and symptoms of **37 US Presidents** from 1776 to 1974 were obtained and given to experienced psychiatrists for classification of mental illness. About half of the Presidents met the criteria for a psychiatric disorder, with **8% meeting the criteria for anxiety disorder**. This research is a bit dodgy, given that it is retrospective, and based on written biographical information rather than formal psychiatric assessment. Nevertheless, I thought it was worth including.

One bright spark decided to investigate if panic attacks were associated with chest pain. Guess what – they are. People with chest pain have a slightly increased risk of panic attacks.[9] The question here, of course, is which one comes first? Do they panic because they've got chest pain, or do they get chest pain because they panic? For our purposes, I think it'd be pretty normal to panic if you actually started out with chest pain; but getting chest pain *because* you're panicking is a different matter.

And here's some news for those of you who have had a panic attack and have also felt the symptoms of depersonalisation or derealisation. You're not alone, because this is quite typical also, with up to 82.6% of patients with panic disorder experiencing these symptoms.[7]

What about certain *personality* types; are certain people predisposed to anxiety and panic? Well, despite the research investigating this issue, the answer is that we don't know.[1] The problem is that if someone with panic or anxiety takes a personality test, the anxiety or panic effects the results of their personality test.

Anyway...what's my point?

Anxiety disorder and panic attacks are common. All sorts of people get anxiety and panic attacks – not just a certain *type*.

So, forget about trying to figure out your anxiety for the moment, and accept this one fact. You are not alone.

Many, many people before you, now, and in the future, have had or will have anxiety disorder and survive it. Not only will they survive it, but they will also come out of it stronger and wiser and their lives will flourish.

3

When panic attacked: My story

I had a rock solid, sound mind. I was very motivated and successful at whatever I put my mind to. I could be very task orientated if necessary, and very gregarious in social environments. I was going conquer my world.

I had a well-developed belief system about the world, the universe, and beyond – and my place within it. I believed in a higher being. I believed that there was a purpose for my life and that I was fulfilling that purpose. I had no sense of vulnerability whatsoever. Of course, I sometimes worried about things, but this was 'surface' worry.

Then, at age 28, I had an unexpected panic attack, and it cut through the surface and went to the centre of my sense of self and destroyed it.

I was at home one Sunday evening talking with my gorgeous wife. We were concerned about something of little consequence. I had also been having increasing doubts about my belief system – doubts about my understanding of the world – and these doubts were becoming insurmountable.

This belief system underpinned my entire way of thinking – and all of a sudden it was gone in what seemed like a flash. It was like removing the operating system on a computer. This wasn't like a software problem that could be corrected by shutting down and starting up again. The operating system was corrupted and none of the software worked.

The best word I can use to describe the panic attack is 'terror'. It was by far the worst experience of my entire life – by orders of magnitude. This panic attack was, and is to a great extent, a defining moment of my life. For a long time afterwards, it was *the* defining moment of my life.

During the attack, I couldn't keep still. Movement, of any kind, provided some sort of cortical distraction – just like how shaking your thumb if you've hurt it somehow makes it feel better. I had to take deep breaths – continuously – the type where if you didn't dig deep enough into the breath, it'd be like you didn't breathe at all.

The other main symptom I had was a 'visceral' or 'gut wrenching' response. Some might describe this as nausea, but it was nothing like the nausea you get when you've got gastritis or feel as if you're going to vomit. It was just the most awful sinking feeling in the pit of my stomach – it was physical dread.

In terms of how this compared to feelings of anxiety I had previously experienced – it didn't. Instead it was a contrast, a stark contrast. Look, here's the fact. Before having had a panic attack, there is no way I could have imagined what it would feel like to have one. Not a chance. If you haven't had a panic attack, you'll just have to take my word for this. If you have had a panic attack, you'll know exactly what I mean.

During the panic attack, I wasn't thinking much. My mind was simply focused on the fear I was experiencing. I didn't know how to relieve the fear.

The worst was over in about 20 minutes, and as the 'edge' came off, I was able to start contemplating what was happening; and there wasn't much 'good' to contemplate…it was all bad…and this didn't help relieve my anxiety.

The panic would come in waves. I'd be able to remain still for a while, until again the panic would come and I would have to roam. This made getting into a car difficult.

"What if I were to panic in the car and I couldn't get out?"

This must have been a real treat for my wife to witness. And here is my tribute to her. **She didn't flinch**. Whether she hid it, or didn't 'understand' the magnitude of what was going on, it doesn't matter. All that matters is that she didn't flinch. She showed no signs of being scared. She didn't patronize me, she didn't try to 'process' me – she was just with me (*and I am forever grateful gorgeous girl*).

I managed to get into the car

I didn't know what to do, but had to do something. After about an hour I was able to risk a car ride. We drove to a friend of ours who was a counsellor. That was a long trip. When we got there, Steve was with another friend and both quickly came to help.

Of course, I was emotional, and was ranting a bit, gushing to explain what was going on. Again, I got lucky. Steve somehow knew what to do – and that was pretty much nothing. The trick to helping me seemed to be, "don't just do something, stand there!"

The other friend, however, thought he might try and 'fix me'. This wasn't a good game plan and most of what he said just made matters worse.

His comments such as, "It'll be OK, you're a smart guy", missed the point entirely.

"Smart, smart, SMART!" I exclaimed, "it's nothing to do with 'smart', it's not intelligence. God, if it was to do with intelligence I wouldn't have this bloody thing. It's not about being *smart*."

He meant well, but Steve quickly shut him up.

Sleep was an amazing remedy. After quite a few hours of intolerable anxiety, I finally went to sleep. I was no longer aware. This was good.

And then I woke up, and within seconds it all came flooding back. The dread, the fear, the gut wrenching nausea – and there was a newcomer that can only be described as 'the opposite of hope, faith, and optimism'. A lot of what happened over the next days and weeks is a bit of a blur. I was unable to attend my university lectures. I was unable to go outside alone. I could manage a walk around the block with my wife, but I couldn't face people. The reason for this is that the anxiety was so overwhelming that I couldn't even fake being normal.

I couldn't have a normal conversation. I either had to be silent, or I had to talk about how anxious I was feeling.

The trip to the GP

After a few days, and with no real change in my symptoms, I went to the local GP. I was given what I now think were the worst two pieces of advice I could have received.

First, I was quickly prescribed a drug (rivotril); and guess what one of the side effects of that drug is? Anxiety.

Rivotril is a benzodiazapine and as you'll find out in chapter 5 they're not all that great. I wasn't told about the possible 'anxiety' side effect by the GP or by the pharmacist. I was given a fairly large bottle and was not scheduled for a follow up visit. It was as simple as, "here you go, have a bottle of Rivotril and be on your way".

Great – you take a drug for anxiety, and it may just give you more anxiety.

What if I got worse on the medication?

Here was my problem: if I remained anxious, or if I became even more anxious while on the medication, or if I became worse after I stopped taking the medication, how would I know if it were *me* that was anxious or the *medication* making me anxious? How would I know if the underlying problem was still a problem, or if I was now anxious as a result of being on the drugs?

I've got to tell you, in the state I was in, the thought of not knowing if it was 'me', or the medication was a trigger for more anxiety.

I couldn't take the drugs.

What about counselling?

The second piece of crap advice I was given was that "counselling doesn't help and is usually a waste of time".

Good one doc. This meant that I wasn't given a referral to a psychologist. I wasn't given any literature on anxiety disorder or panic attacks. No explanation. Nothing except the rivotril.

To be honest, I was cautious about seeing a counsellor or psychologist because if they didn't understand where I was coming from, or if they began to try and process me by questioning the very fragile hold that I had on life, this might have sent me over the edge.

I could only talk to people I knew and trusted and who were wise enough not to try and process me or explain it all away with pithy, superficial pop-psychology.

At that time, my wife was working out of town in a regional hospital, and so for the first week I stayed with my 'counsellor' friend, who was simply supportive and didn't try to process me. In fact, he was sick at home – which meant he *couldn't* even try to process me.

I then decided to go and stay with my wife, which was my first real attempt at encountering the world again. She was staying in a dormitory with a parade of other visiting health professionals, which meant that I had to interact with a whole bunch of strangers who would politely try to engage me in small talk. And it was an unfamiliar environment.

Depersonalization

This is when I really began to notice a new symptom, which goes by the name depersonalization.

"Oh, great" I thought with a touch of sarcasm – and I was getting good at sarcasm. "Fantastic. This is just getting better and better."

"How about on top of fear, anxiety, nausea, the loss of hope and the risk of insanity, why not throw another bizarre symptoms on the pile? You know, really immerse yourself in this Nic. You are a star."

So, I began to experience the feeling that I was *observing myself* going about my day, especially if I was interacting with people. It wasn't like I was watching a movie of myself, so it wasn't a visual experience. It was a detached experience, but wasn't an out of body experience. It was a change in perspective.

I was the observer rather than the doer. The doer was my 'physical body' moving, talking, and eating. But I was the observer – the alone, anxious observer. I wasn't 'in' the moment; I was anxiously observing the moment. I was anxiously 'self-aware'.

This was very boring. It was frustrating. I hated this feeling. Anxiety was a normal experience that I had experienced before and was now experiencing excessively as panic attacks and anxiety disorder – but depersonalization was a completely new experience for me and was completely unfamiliar.

Going out for dinner?

We all went out for dinner and I was sitting next to a doctor who worked at the hospital. Again, because the anxiety was so intense, it was all I could do to stop myself saying to this guy, "my God…if only you knew how I was feeling right now while I'm listening to you".

Of course it didn't make matters any better when he started telling me that his evenings in the emergency department always dragged on because that's when "all the crazies" came out.

So, now I was thinking "I feel like I a normal person who is experiencing something bizarre that is beyond my control, that I didn't ask for, and that would earn me the prestigious title of 'crazy' if I turned up to your emergency department at night. OK. Note to self, don't go to the emergency department."

You see, if you start with a panic attack, and add ongoing anxiety to this, plus a loss of hope and the sense of depersonalization, and add to that the lack of an obvious treatment plus some fear about medication and fear about going insane, then you end up with a lot of anxiety and fear of the future.

Panic attack + abnormal anxiety + loss of hope + depersonalization + no obvious treatment I could take + no sense of when or if this would ever be over + normal anxiety in response to these experiences = a whole lot of anxiety.

I can still remember the long train journey back to the city – alone. I was aware of every second of that trip. Stuck on a train, by myself, not sure what the hell was going on or what would happen. No apparent options. Negative self-talk. Feeling stuck and as if I needed to jump off the train, then scared I *would* jump off the train. I finally made it home.

I had also noticed another strange symptom. I couldn't look at myself in the mirror – specifically, I couldn't look into my own eyes. I would purposefully drop my head whenever I was near a mirror. I don't know how long this went on for – but it was months.[1]

Anyway, back to the story

After about another week with no improvement I decided to try more specialised help and got myself a referral to a psychiatrist. The psychiatrist was a friend of a friend, and so I had some reason to trust that it would all be OK.

He practiced from his home, and so I drove through a beautiful, green leafy suburb and parked outside the front a very nice house – heart pounding. To get to his office I had to walk down the side of the house and around the back. There was a waiting room, and the last thing I wanted to do was to sit in a waiting room with other people who were waiting to see the PSYCHIATRIST!

The fact that I might see other people who had 'mental' problems was enough to set off my anxiety. "This wasn't me – what on earth am I doing here – I'm not the type of person to need a psychiatrist!" I had to wait and fill out a form, all the while with a terrible feeling in my gut that was only somewhat relieved by a deep breath. I took a lot of deep breaths – but even then, I didn't want to sit there taking too many obvious deep breaths; so I had to take slow, long deep breaths – keeping up appearances you know.

---

1 Of course, now I can gaze lovingly at myself for hours…

Funnily enough, it was in his waiting room that I discovered that slow and deep abdominal breathing helped to reduce my feelings of anxiety – at least a little bit. But no-one else had told me this little tip.

The psychiatrist

The psych was nice enough. Didn't say much – which was good really. At least he wasn't giving me bad news, like "you're insane and need to be committed".

His prognosis was, however, depressing, and went something like this:

"Most people with anxiety will always have anxiety, especially if they have Panic Disorder. But, most people cope and live normal lives as long as they take their medication. Here's a sample pack of Zoloft. Take this when you get home and I'll see you next week".

He gave me some other advice of a general nature, I parted with a significant sum of money, and then I was on my way – Zoloft in hand.

"Gosh", I thought, "I gave him the diagnosis so he didn't have to work for that, and his solution was as simple as handing out a sample pack of Zoloft; but he hasn't told me what is wrong with me and why I'm having these attacks".

I knew that I was anxious and panicky – that's why I went – but I wanted to know how to get things back to normal. Maybe it was denial, but I didn't want drugs, I didn't want time out, I didn't want to analyse my childhood – I just wanted things to be back to normal, pronto.

I didn't take the Zoloft.

I often looked at the packet, but I didn't take it. Again, I was concerned that if I took the pills and felt better, that it would be a 'false' better, and that 'I' would not be better; and damn it, I wanted to be better.

And Zoloft comes with it's own little secrets – well they're not secrets, but they are side effects. After reading the little writing on the information sheet, I just couldn't take it – at that time the risk of side-effects was small, but were still too great. At least for now, I hadn't gone mad, got worse, or tried to end it all – and that was better than the risks posed by taking Zoloft.

At this point I have to be very careful and respectful to those who have decided to take medication. We each experience and respond to anxiety differently, we each have a different perspective, different knowledge, and different lives. And remember, there are different types of anxiety disorder. For me, however, the thought of taking medication, and the potential consequences of that, was a trigger for anxiety. I therefore did what most people do who are anxious – I avoided the trigger.

I was debilitated. I could hardly get up the courage to go outside. It was even difficult paying bills on the telephone with a computerised assistant! I woke up in the morning and felt panicked, and then continued to feel panicked until I managed to get off to sleep again that night. Even though I didn't want to take the medication, I can empathize with those who *do* decide to take medication. I carried it around in my bag for about 4 years.

So, off I go to the PSYCHIATRIST the following week – same house, same room, same quietly spoken gentlemen, whose main interest, after flicking through his notes while trying to remember me, was "**did you take the medication**"?

I answered "**No**".

It was like he came to life. His eyebrows raised; he sat up in his chair; he became animated; and for a brief moment actually looked concerned. I tried to explain myself. He told me to take the medication. I said I would.

I didn't take the medication.

I didn't see him again. He'd done all he could do – he gave me pills. He had nothing else to offer. It was all up to me.

What happened next?

As time went on, I told a few more people. I was quite concerned about what people would think of me, and so I always prefaced the news with an explanation that I knew anxiety was weird and potentially awkward for people to deal with. This way I hoped I could put them at ease so that they would respond to me, rather than react to me.

I told some friend's. I told my father and mother. They did their best to understand. I was studying at the time, and told two academic staff members – both of whom were understanding and did not make me feel somehow 'less of a person'.

I had become so close to the edge that the very thought of sitting in a small room to talk about 'anxiety' with some-one I didn't know, and therefore didn't trust, was actually a trigger for my anxiety. I was now no-where near being able to analyse it. I just needed to get through the day.

At that stage, being able to focus on something other than the anxiety was essential to my final recovery.

I will always be thankful to Sinefield who provided regular evening reprieves with his hilarious sit-com, which I found very funny.

How did people react?

For the most part, the people who I told about my anxiety did OK with the news; but there are only so many people you can tell, and of those you tell, there are only so many times that you can tell them how you're feeling.

So, I soon stopped telling people. I stopped talking about it – and this was a good thing in retrospect. My thoughts were already magnetized to my anxiety and talking about it all the time to anyone who would listen would have been counter-productive.

I'd discovered some techniques that helped reduce the severity of the attacks, and so I also didn't feel as compelled to talk about them. But I can tell you that it's quite weird and unpleasant to go about your day-to-day life interacting with people as if you're normal and happy when in fact you're anxiously observing the whole thing at a distance – not part of the moment. It's lonely.

I did need someone on this planet who cared about me to know that I was feeling absolutely awful – otherworldly awful. And I needed them to 'get it'; that it wasn't just "oh, I'm feeling a bit down about whatever" or "I'm feeling really nervous about my exams". I needed them to get that what I was feeling was anxiety amplified beyond my belief, that

I was not experiencing normal anxiety but anxiety beyond words.

So words weren't what I needed to hear from anyone, because despite their best efforts, their words would trivialise the magnitude of the situation. Lucky for me I had an angel. She didn't know how bad it was but she knew it was bad.

I just had to look at her, or squeeze her hand and whisper, "I'm feeling anxious" and the edge would come off; enough so that I could keep on walking, or sitting, or...living. Just the fact that someone else knew that I wasn't feeling normal was a great relief.

So, if you're reading this and you've never had an anxiety attack or suffered from anxiety disorder, then consider this. Let your friend, lover, family member, or whomever it is that you know has anxiety disorder, tell you that they are anxious. Accept that even though the stimulus for the anxiety might seem trivial to you – and it might seem trivial to them for that matter – that the fear, dread or terror they are feeling is real nonetheless.

Then, avoid trying to process them (unless you have their permission).

It may not be useful to explain why they shouldn't be anxious. They are probably well aware of the fact that there's no need to be anxious – and this is probably making them all the more anxious. So, just listen and accept them. If you're not with them, it might help if you called them every now and then to ask how they're going – but check this with them first, because calling them and asking might just be a trigger for their anxiety!

A year down the track

After about a year, I'd figured out how to stop having panic attacks. I'd had enough of them to know that nothing much eventuated from them and so I wasn't as concerned by them. I just got on with it.

But I had developed generalised anxiety disorder and lived with a fairly constant feeling of baseline anxiety that would rarely, if ever, dissipate. Instead, it would swell if I encountered certain triggers. By using various techniques that I had discovered, such as deep breathing, it would then ease back to the baseline anxiety. It certainly seemed like this was how it was going to be forever.

During this period, that first panic attack was *the* defining moment of my life. It seemed that everything in my life grew from that moment in time when panic attacked.

Figuring out the triggers

Trying to figure out what was triggering my anxiety wasn't easy. I was aware of certain triggers from the start, but it seemed that other things would trigger my anxiety, and I didn't know why – and it's hard to avoid triggers when you don't really know what they are, where they're hiding, or when they're going to strike.

I later learned that fear can become *conditioned* to show up in response to non-threatening triggers – triggers that may only somewhat resemble the original trigger of your fear. And then there are just panic attacks that come on for no apparent reason whatsoever – and you can drive yourself 'mad' trying to figure it all out.

Anyway, this is where anxiety disorder becomes unique to the individual. I didn't have a specific phobia about heights, or dogs, open spaces or closed spaces – so none of these things triggered my anxiety.

Instead, certain thoughts, or rather questions, were triggers for my anxiety – and these damn questions just wouldn't leave me alone.

If I said to you, "don't think of a pink elephant", the very thing you would think about would be pink elephants. And the more you try not to think about pink elephants, the more you probably think of pink elephants.

As soon as I had 'nothing on my mind', these questions would be on my mind. This is why, for me, engaging in cognitive activities, like reading or studying, would keep me occupied. Being stuck somewhere with nothing to do wasn't a good idea – those questions would come and 'get me'; and when they came they were damn hard to get rid of.

Thankfully I have far more control of my thoughts these days, and it's been fascinating for me to reflect on the thoughts that would trigger my anxiety. There were definitely underlying themes.

If I were to think of a body function, like breathing, or carbon dioxide regulation, or kidney function, or gastro-intestinal function, I would begin to feel overwhelmed by this knowledge in my head, and would start to panic.

I would feel anxious if I were to think, "imagine if you had to actually concentrate on breathing in order to breathe".

I knew that I didn't have to concentrate on breathing in order to breath, and I wasn't scared that I would stop breathing if I didn't concentrate – but the thought of having to concentrate on it would make me anxious.

Whereas before, I was able to engage in thought experiments about life and the universe, now I couldn't. I used to be able to discuss topics such as 'knowledge', 'epistemology', and 'meta-physics', but these subjects became taboo for me.

There were certain *questions* that would occupy my mind that I just couldn't ask myself anymore – but my mind would keep returning to these damn questions. There were no answers to the questions, and so it was pointless asking them.

I also discovered that it wasn't specific 'knowledge' that made me anxious; it was the self-awareness about my 'knowledge' that was a trigger. If I became self aware, I'd immediately become anxious. I longed for periods of just being, or doing, without being aware of myself, because 'myself' was anxious.

Ridiculous triggers

Holding a belief that was false, or potentially false, was also a trigger for anxiety. For example, I was on a farm, and the farmer commented that the sheep had moved from one end of the paddock to the other end, and then provided a reason for why they had done this. My anxiety was immediately triggered, because I thought, "he doesn't really know why the sheep moved"; and the main trigger was that he *didn't seem to know that he didn't know.*

Now if this isn't an example of an overactive error-detection system I don't know what is!

I mean, really, getting highly anxious over some sheep in a paddock is completely ridiculous.

And I ***knew*** it was ridiculous. But this didn't stop me feeling anxious, it made me more anxious – and of course once you start feeling anxious, you become self aware and all the fears and concerns you have about anxiety fill your head and you spiral toward a panic attack.

I became anxious around people who were so sure that what they 'knew' was 'true'. I couldn't watch movies about people with blind faith. I couldn't watch movies that included religion. I couldn't watch TV shows about history because I knew that a lot of what people 'knew' to be 'true' in the past had then turned out to be 'wrong' in the 'future', and the thought of this was a trigger for my anxiety.

Gullibility also made me anxious. So, I might have been sitting on a bus, and seen a mother and child, and thought about how vulnerable that child's mind was to accepting, as true, the information provided by the mother that may be incorrect; and this thought would trigger anxiety.

"Deep breath", I'd think. "It's just a Mum with her child. Deep breath…"

Of course I understood that uncertainty was actually the reality of every human being who has ever lived. But, again, knowing this didn't reduce my anxiety. Of course I understood that uncertainty was the way of the world, and that nothing would ever change. I also knew that uncertainty had never made me anxious before.

And this is the very reason why anxiety disorder is different from plain old worry or anxiety. It doesn't necessarily make sense. I knew it didn't make sense, and this, of course was worrying. It was normal to be anxious about the fact that I was abnormally anxious.

Remember:

Abnormal anxiety PLUS normal anxiety about having abnormal anxiety EQUALS a lot of anxiety!

Arrogance

One night, I was alone in the kitchen. I was standing at the sink washing dishes. It was a Sunday night, and there was a jazz music station broadcasting a story on the roots of gospel music. They played a gospel song sung by slaves, and the lyrics were based on a faith in God and they were optimistic about the future – if not the future on earth, then the future in heaven.

I thought to myself pessimistically about the hopeless situation these people were in: "what did they know back then"? The *thought* that these people had false hope – that what they believed to be true in such dire circumstances may have been incorrect – made me anxious. Those slaves probably died as slaves and never saw the optimistic future they were singing about. Imagine spending all this time thinking and singing about a good future, when in fact, there was no good future for them. Imagining this made me highly anxious.

But then it occurred to me, "well, what the hell do **you** know"? What do you know about anything, Nic

Lucas? Sure, you've been to uni and know some stuff – big deal – there's a stack more stuff that you don't know, so don't get self-righteous and think that you know more than people in the past – 'cause in the big scheme of things, you don't. You schmuck."

Funnily enough, this was a huge relief. First, I found it funny to tell myself off. Second, I realised that I had placed upon myself an expectation that being educated meant that I 'knew stuff' about the world, and I had fallen for my own publicity. I had It may seem like a small incident – but it makes it into this story as one of my key emotional turning points. All of a sudden I felt incredibly humble. This was a good feeling, and I liked good feelings, so I stayed with the humility for quite a while.

Uncertainty

It was from this experience that I became far less anxious of uncertainty. It was from this experience that I became no longer scared about finding out that something I believed in turned out to be wrong. It didn't matter. In fact, it became a source of amusement to me, to find out that I was wrong, We only learn and get closer to the truth when we find out and acknowledge that something we believed was either completely wrong, or at least not quite right.

I have a quote on my desk that says,

"When an honest person who is mistaken hears the truth, they either cease to be mistaken, or they cease to be honest".[1]

Such a simple quote, but it hit home when I first read it.

The next phase

When I first experienced a panic attack, it was terrifying. I was then, naturally, terrified that it would happen again. I was also concerned that I was losing my mind and I was scared of losing everything I loved.

Then I learned how to stop having panic attacks and entered the more 'generalised anxiety disorder' phase, where I had constant feelings of anxiety – from the moment I woke up until the moment I went to sleep.

This was depressing, and it would have been easy for me to come to the conclusion that this was it; that for the rest of my life I would experience this appalling feeling – a feeling that I described as the *opposite of life*.

The next phase of my recovery, however, was the realisation that I *could* have moments where I did not experience anxiety and I *could* have moments when I was not self-aware. This realisation gave me a sense of hope that I hadn't had for many months.

The 'Bus' story

Around this time I remember sitting on a bus, running late for an appointment. I had that sinking feeling in my stomach, and after a while I realized that, "I've got that sinking feeling in my stomach". This meant that I *hadn't been aware* of the sinking feeling in my stomach. I also realized that it was normal to have that sinking feeling in my stomach; after all, I was running late for something important.

And I can't tell you the relief. "Normal anxiety! **Break out the bubbly** – I'm anxious and it's normal!"

So there I was, sitting on the bus, feeling anxious about my lateness and finding it hard to wipe the smile off my face. ***Anxious but Happy***. Now that was a major turning point. That was when I really knew that feeling normal again was possible, and I gradually experienced more and more moments without anxiety.

If I realised, however, that I hadn't been feeling anxious for a few hours, then this self-awareness would trigger the anxiety. This was hard work, but as time past and my confidence grew, I discovered different techniques and strategies that helped me to reduce my anxious feelings. Eventually, I was able to read about anxiety and begin to try and understand it without feeling anxious. In fact, I can still remember the day when I pulled a psychology textbook from the bookshelf and read the formal description of anxiety. I'd been aware of that book on my bookshelf for about two years before I felt I was able to open it up.

I had anxiety for a few more years – but it became less and less intense and less and less frequent. I was able to tolerate certain triggers or cues that I had not been able to tolerate for years – and sometimes I would be doing something without remembering that it used to be a trigger. I would go for days without feeling anxious, and then this turned into weeks. It then turned into years and at the time of writing I haven't had abnormal anxiety for over 7 years now. I've had some 'normal anxiety' but this hasn't been problematic.

Instead of that first panic attack being *the* defining moment of my life, it is now just *one* of the defining moments of my life.

What am I doing now?

Now I write about anxiety disorders and panic attacks for the purpose of helping other people and I welcome opportunities to speak to groups of people.

It's important for men to speak out about their experiences with anxiety, because even though it's twice as common in women, there are still many, many men who suffer in silence – and they need support, they need hope, and they need options.

There were a lot of techniques and strategies that I discovered along the way that helped me conquer panic attacks, and then anxiety. Perhaps if I had tried formal therapy, I might have learned these techniques earlier and improved more quickly, but I didn't, and so it was up to me to learn how to overcome anxiety disorder by myself: self-help.

When I first began to write this book, I specifically refrained from giving much detail about the strategies I had discovered and personally used to overcome panic attacks and anxiety. The reason for not writing about these was that I had no evidence or proof that what I had discovered would be of any use to anyone else.

And evidence is important to me – anyone can get up and 'crap on', and I didn't want to be one of those.

Remember, I didn't go to a psychologist or counsellor and so I have no experience of 'formal therapy'. I was concerned that what I would describe and that the strategies I had used may have seemed silly or considered useless in comparison to formally recognised therapies.

Also, since I am not a qualified psychologist or counsellor, I was cautious about offering suggestions or strategies for overcoming panic and anxiety. My plan was to write a book about anxiety, who get's it, what's going on in the brain, what formal treatments are available, and what the scientific evidence is for their effectiveness. I also, hesitantly, decided to include my story.

I had hoped that this information would provide other people with a resource that would encourage and inspire them to overcome anxiety and panic, just as I had done.

But then I did the research for chapter 5 of this book,

the chapter on the treatments for anxiety and the evidence for their effectiveness. And after doing that research I realised there *was* room for me to write about the strategies and techniques that I had discovered and successfully used.

So, I decided to write down and describe the techniques I had used to overcome panic attacks and anxiety disorder and I've put that together in a manual to be read in conjunction with this book, called it:

From Anxious to Happy: A manual for overcoming anxiety and panic attacks.

If you don't have this manual already, it is available at www.fromanxioustohappy.com

I am not claiming that the strategies I discovered are unique – in fact, most of what I discovered could be labelled under some formal type of therapy.

What I do claim, however, is that the information included in the manual is authentic.

It really worked for me and there is scientific proof that it has also worked for other people (see Chapter 5 on the evidence for Self-Help).

Anyway…I hope that after reading my story you feel in some way 'better'. If you feel inspired to overcome anxiety then I've succeeded. If you feel relieved because you've discovered that someone else like me has experienced anxiety and panic like you, then I've also accomplished something. In the next chapter, I explain the basic gist of what's going on in the **brain** when you've got anxiety, because understanding how the **brain** works during anxiety helped me learn how to reduce my anxiety.

The anxiety 'server': A brief look at the brain

Every day, thousands of people search the internet for information on anxiety – and if I had to guess I'd say it was because searching the internet is discreet. You can search for and buy information online about anxiety without having to make a public 'admission' that you're looking at that stuff. So, since this book was most likely going to be bought on the internet, I decided that I'd approach this chapter using the **Internet** as an analogy for our brain and our experiences.

Most of our conscious awareness occurs in our 'cortex'. This is the grey stuff (grey matter) that forms the surface of our brain. It's where you experience things that are created by deeper brain structures. You actually experience *vision* with your cortex, not with your eyes. You hear with your cortex, smell with your cortex, taste with your cortex and feel (touch and emotion) with your cortex.

So, your cortex is where you *experience* things; it's where you have an awareness of what's going on in your deeper brain structures. In this way, your cortex is like a computer screen that displays web pages for you to experience – and understanding where these web pages come from will help you to understand anxiety a little better.

Where 'are' web pages?

The actual web pages that you experience are not stored on your computer screen, or even on your computer:[2] they are stored on a 'server' somewhere else. A 'sever' is just a name for another computer which 'serves' the web pages to your computer screen – just like your deep brain structures 'serve' your visual or emotional experiences to your cortex.

Just where are those servers?

When it comes to surfing the Internet, does anyone have a clue where those 'servers' actually are? Not really… they could be anywhere. They are hidden. Intangible. All we see are the web pages, and most of us don't really know how it all works. We don't need to know how it works in order to 'see' and 'experience' web pages; though we sure do get annoyed if the pages don't display properly.[3]

Dynamic Web Pages

Have you noticed that on many web pages there is some text at the bottom of the page that says, "last updated on…". What this tells you is that web pages are not static – but that they can be changed or modified so that when they are 'served' to your computer screen they display differently. A different banner perhaps, or different text, graphics or layout. Many web pages are now interac-

2 Except, of course, if they're stored in your cache file, but let's not complicate things…

3 I, of course, always keep calm and never get frustrated by such things ☺

tive, and you can enter information, buy products, or link through to other web pages.

Web pages can contain hidden 'code' that records what you do while you're looking at the page (e.g. how long you stayed on the page, what links you selected) and this information is reported back to the 'server'. In response to this, the server can 'change' which web pages it serves to you.

An active web user

Now, instead of just being a 'passive surfer' of the Internet, let's consider that you're an 'active user': you have *your* own web page and you want the world to see it.

In order for the world to be able to 'see and experience' your web page, you have to load it up to a 'server'. Now, you know how to view web pages online, but do you know how to send web pages in the other direction – from your computer to the 'server' and for the world to see?

The most common method is what is called 'file transfer protocol', or FTP for short.

You use an FTP program to upload or transfer the web pages you create from your computer to the 'server', and once it's there, anyone can view and experience the file as a web page. So, there's a two way street between your computer and the server. It can send stuff to you – and you can send stuff to it.

OK, so what does all this have to do anxiety?

The computer screen is an analogy for your cortex – the surface grey matter that covers your brain.

You have a stack of other grey matter though, and it sits deep in your brain – scattered all over the place in discrete 'areas'. These areas of deep brain grey matter are called 'nuclei'; but instead of calling them that, I'm calling them 'servers'.

Your 'awareness' or your 'consciousness' is like the computer screen and your deep brain nuclei are the servers, which serve up what we 'experience'.

By experience I mean all that we see, hear, smell, taste, and feel – both touch and emotion.

Did you get that last bit? Feel – **emotionally**.

For many years now we've known that what we 'feel' emotionally is served up to us – to our cortex – from our 'servers' or deep brain nuclei.

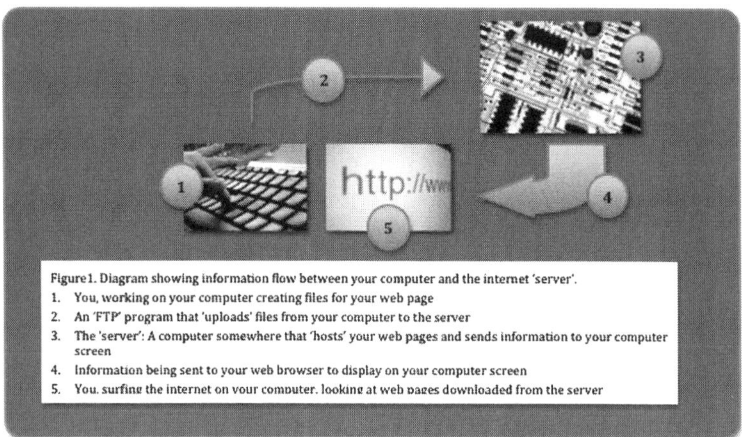

Figure 1. Diagram showing information flow between your computer and the internet 'server'.

1. You, working on your computer creating files for your web page
2. An 'FTP' program that 'uploads' files from your computer to the server
3. The 'server': A computer somewhere that 'hosts' your web pages and sends information to your computer screen
4. Information being sent to your web browser to display on your computer screen
5. You. surfing the internet on your computer. looking at web pages downloaded from the server

Feeling happy?

This emotion is served up to your cortex like a happy web page and you get to experience it. Do you know where the server is? No. Do you know how it works? No. Does it matter? No, You're just happy.

Feeling anxious? Feeling scared? Feeling panicky?

When we're feeling these less enjoyable emotions – especially if they are interfering with our daily lives – the answers should be different. It probably doesn't matter if we know 'where' the server is, but it does become important to know 'how it works'. If we know how it works, then we can try and modify which web pages are displayed and what is displayed on them.

We can try and modify what we experience.

By analogy, we also need to learn which web sites to visit (e.g. which thoughts to have). Some web sites are just no good for us and we need to stay away.

It's like we need 'parental control' software for our own brains to block us from thinking or dwelling on certain things.

We can attempt to do this ourselves, using various psychological techniques. Drugs also work in this way. They artificially block certain emotions from being experienced and artificially allow other emotions to be experienced.

We also need to learn how to change or edit our own web pages and 'up load' these edited versions to our brain servers by using some sort of FTP program. There are lots of 'brain FTP programs' around for you to try. Cognitive behavioural therapy is one FTP approach. Hypnosis is another. Some people use neurolinguistic programming (NLP), and others use prayer or meditation.

The aim of each of these techniques is to change the experiences we have. To change how we respond to certain triggers. To change how we think about certain issues. To correct misunderstandings and identify the false logic (code for bull crap) that often bangs around inside our heads.

Many people who have anxiety disorder are great thinkers – and they need to learn how to think their way out of anxiety.

Many people who have anxiety disorder are great thinkers – and they need to learn how to think their way out of anxiety.

Right about now, some of you are probably thinking, "Oh what a bunch of crap. You're trying to tell me that if I just 'think' positive thoughts, or choose not to feel anxious, that I'll get over this".

Well, no – I'm not saying that, and it's certainly not that simple.

Consider this…

Remember when the Internet first started, and we all had dial-up accounts (many people still do have dial up accounts!) Dial up accounts are slow right? So, you understand the concept that there are *different* rates of file transfer. You might also have heard of bandwidth? Bandwidth is simply how much data, per second, can be sent along a certain pathway.

And here's the challenge for us. The information flow from our emotional servers to our cortex is very, very fast. Not only is it fast, it is expansive. There are estimated to be about seven times more neurons carrying information from our emotional (limbic) servers to our cortex than the other way around. Seven times!

When our servers 'serve' us up a dose of emotion, we are wired to go along for the ride – we are wired to experience the emotion. We are not wired to analyse and modify the emotion. Think about it. We are in the plains of Southern Africa and have become the potential feast of a hungry lion. We see the lion, but before 'we see' the lion, our deep brain servers for fear and survival have already 'seen' the lion and have increased our heart rate and opened up the arteries in our leg muscles so that we can run like hell! We're not meant to stand and think, "hmmm…now why is my heart racing", or "I wonder if I can think positive thoughts to reduce my heart rate".

This fear or anxiety response is a useful and normal response. The same kind of response happens if your superannuation fund has dropped in value by 50%. In fact, the same response can happen even if you're scared that your superannuation fund might drop in value by 50%!

Sometimes we're more scared about what might happen than we are when it actually happens. And this is because fear is first and foremost an *early warning system*. It's supposed to help you prevent something bad from happening, and in this way it's a bit like pain. But I digress…

When you consider your panic attacks, or anxiety, ask yourself these questions, "What is the system warning you about" and "what is it trying to prevent"?

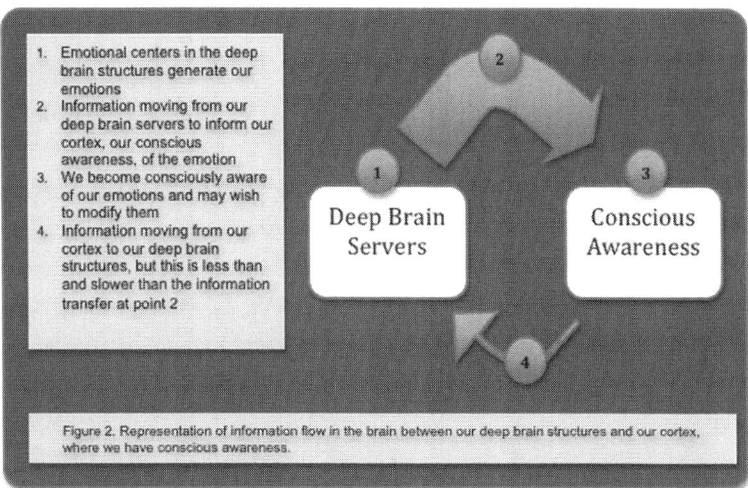

Figure 2. Representation of information flow in the brain between our deep brain structures and our cortex, where we have conscious awareness.

And then ask, "Has this bad thing ever happened – even though I've been scared of it".

The reason for these questions is that for many people, the very things that they are panicking about *never happen*. Someone might be anxious about vomiting in public. They may get so concerned about it that when they are in public, they feel like they are going to vomit – and then they panic.

But then, the panic passes, and guess what? They didn't vomit. They survived it.

Worrying about things that don't happen

Some people (like I was) are anxious about having an obvious panic attack in public – but never have an obvious panic attack in public. Some people get anxious and feel that they are having a heart attack – but as it turns out, there is nothing wrong with their heart and they never have a heart attack.

Sooner or later, you realise that the things you fear in relation to your panic attacks just don't seem to happen. Even though your *early warning system* is going off, it seems to be a false alarm. Sooner or later, you just have to start questioning your early warning system – and maybe even learn to ignore it.

Even if you're concerned about the actual panic attack itself – the simple question is, "what's the worst thing that has ever happened when you've had a panic attack"?

Sure panic attacks are awful, but if you've had panic attacks in the past, and nothing bad has happened as a result, then sooner or later you can stop fearing the panic attacks because nothing happens.

They come. They're awful. They go, and you're still there.

Conditioning

One of the theories underlying panic attacks is something they call ***conditioning***. Your anxiety or panic becomes *conditioned* to show up whenever you encounter a certain trigger – and the trigger could be quite arbitrary.

Many people are familiar with conditioning, and it was first described by a guy called Pavlov. He trained his dogs to salivate at the sound of a bell. He started by always sounding the bell when he gave them food, but after a while, even the sound of the bell would cause the dogs to salivate.

It is well established that humans demonstrate *conditioning* also.

So, maybe you're scared of vomiting. Maybe you vomited once in public, felt embarrassed and have been scared of it happening again. Now, every time you feel nauseas, you get anxious, because you're scared you may vomit.

So, you're sitting on a plane, and the plane hit's some turbulence, and for a second, you become aware of your stomach – **but that's all your *early warning system* needs – a split second.**

You've been conditioned to become anxious at the slightest *gut* sensation, and so you dutifully and predictably become anxious – even though you're not nauseas and you're not going to vomit.

This is a description of how your deep brain servers interpret a visceral/gut sensation as representing a threat, and then serve up a dose of panic for you to experience. You may be experiencing a happy web page, but all of a sudden you get re-directed to a panic web page – and not only that you might have **100 pop-up windows** of that panic web page appear and it may cause your real browser (your brain) to crash.

The good news about conditioning, though, is that it can be reversed. Back to the dogs: if, after a while, the bell is never accompanied by food, the effect of the bell wears off and the dogs no longer salivate when they hear it. Quite a few psychological techniques for the treatment of anxiety, such as graded exposure and virtual reality, are designed to reverse this kind of conditioning.

It's also one of the methods used to help people overcome a phobia. For example, if someone has a phobia of spiders, graded exposure may mean that at first they practice sitting with a picture of a spider on a table on the other side of the room. Then, when they can handle that, they may sit in a room with a spider in a box, situated at the other end of the room. Then they gradually practice sitting closer to the spider in the box – and on it goes, until eventually they can be in the room with the spider and not feel anxious (or least feel less anxious)

Before I move onto the next section of this chapter, it's probably a good idea to summarise the main points so far.

First, your cortex is where you **experience everything** – including anxiety and panic.

Second, those experiences are created and then served up to your cortex **from deep brain servers**.

Third, these deep brain servers have superhighways of information going to your cortex, but your cortex has a narrow one-way street going back to these servers – so you are **wired to go along for the ride** with your emotions, not the other way around.

Fourth, the deep brain servers can become *conditioned* to serve you up a dose of emotion at the **slightest hint of a threat**. In fact, they may become so over-sensitive that they even interpret some non-threatening stimuli as threatening – so you get a hefty dose of 'warning' in the form of anxiety or panic, and you don't understand why your servers served it up to you.

Fifth, even though there's only a narrow one-way street of information going back to your servers, you can try and **up-load improved information to the servers** in order to modify what they, in turn, send back to your cortex.

The point of learning all this is to understand that you're still OK. You're not going crazy, and you're not losing your mind.

Your deep brain servers have become sensitised and over active and you need to learn how to control them and quieten them down.

So, let's take a closer look at these deep brain servers.

The Deep Brain Servers

First, I want to start with a few questions.

Is your 'toe' you? Is your 'elbow' you? And here's a slightly more personal one – is your **'tongue'** you?

How you answer this will depend on your knowledge, understanding, perspective, and belief system[4] – but there's a few general points I'd like to make.

First, you still exist if you lost your toe. In fact, you'd still exist if you lost your tongue. **Second**, make no mistake, if you lost either your toe or your tongue you would experi-

4 In fact, this is a highly debated philosophical question. Imagine if your whole body could be replaced, or if certain parts of your brain could be replaced – when would you cease to be you and become something else?

ence disability as a result; life wouldn't be as easy and you would have to learn a new way of 'being'.

OK, next question. Is your amygdala you?

"Huh…what's an amygdala?

Pronounced *a-myg-da-la*, this is a very tiny bit of grey matter deep in your brain that has some pretty amazing and useful functions. Just like a computer 'server', this bit of grey matter hosts survival instincts, like cleanliness and safety, and also fear and rage. And just like your toe, when something goes wrong with it life isn't as easy as it was.

The amygdala is part of the *limbic* system – a system that is involved in processing and creating emotional experiences for us, including anxiety. Your cortex, like a computer screen, displays the emotions sent to it by the 'server'.

The amygdala, however, is only a very small part of your brain; it is only one of many servers and it does not sum 'you' up. This is good news.

The somewhat challenging news is that the limbic system has a far greater impact on your consciousness – your awareness of anxiety – than your consciousness has on the limbic system. This is desirable, in fact, in situations where fear and anxiety are appropriate responses, such as when running for your life from a tiger, or from the paparazzi for that matter.

This system is not so great, however, when anxiety is *not* an appropriate response for the situation, or is no longer useful.

Real time pictures of brain function have revealed that there are about 7 times more neurones going from the limbic system to your cortex than there are going from your cortex to the limbic system.[10] And this is where you're kind of outnumbered. You're going along for the emotional ride, whether you like it or not. If the limbic system get's anxious, then hold on, there's a rough time ahead.

When something is up with the limbic system, the person it belongs to can experience various kinds of emotional upheaval.

Functional brain imaging studies are being increasingly used to measure the activity of brain structures, or regions, during different emotional states. The basic gist of these studies is to record brain function in those who suffer with anxiety disorder and compare this with people who do not have anxiety disorder.

Some researchers go as far as to induce feelings of anxiety in the group of people with anxiety disorder and the group of people without anxiety disorder, while measuring their brain function. They measure those parts of the brain are active and how active they become, and then compare the findings between the anxiety group and the non-anxiety group.

It should come as no surprise to those of you who have suffered from anxiety or panic attacks that **your brain** does, indeed, function differently compared to people who are not suffering from anxiety. While this might seem obvious, it has been important to verify this with scientific studies because sometimes what would seem to be obvious turns out to be wrong.

So, the brain imaging studies are there to help us understand *how* anxiety works and *where* it is all going on.

From the available information, it appears that the parts of the brain that regulate *normal* fear responses in *normal* people have become over-active in people with anxiety and panic attacks.

While the triggers for anxiety or panic can vary widely between people, the over-excited fear pathways in the brain create the anxiety or panic that is common amongst people with anxiety disorder.

There are a large number of *alterations* in the nervous systems of people with anxiety disorder, including **changes** in the microscopic structure of some nerve cells, **changes** in the receptors – or aerials – that sit on the walls of nerve cells, and **changes** in the amounts of various chemicals that hook up to these receptors.

The Fear Pathways

To begin, let's take a brief look at the actual 'fear' servers – the little nuclei or groups of nerve cells that are involved in the fear pathways.

Etkin, a professor from the Stanford Medical School, has suggested that these overactive 'fear pathways' are the common link between a variety of disorders including anxiety, phobias, and post-traumatic stress disorder. Etkin and colleagues[11] examined all of the available brain imaging studies and found that while multiple brain regions were over active in those with panic attacks and anxiety disorder, the amygdala and insula (another 'server') were the most commonly involved.

In people with obsessive-compulsive disorder they also found an overactive link between the front of the brain and the fear and survival pathways.

In addition to knowing that the various regions of the brain are overactive, there is also a stack of research on *alterations* in the various chemicals that are released by nerves that regulate the fear pathways. In each of the anxiety disorders, changes have been observed in serotonin pathways, GABA pathways, dopamine pathways, and adrenaline pathways.

In addition to these, people with obsessive-compulsive disorder also have changes in various neuropeptides – the proteins in the nervous system that tell nerves to do stuff.

This is fascinating research,

as it does demonstrate physiological or 'real' changes in brain function in those with anxiety disorder. It is a fact that anxiety disorders aren't just 'in the mind' but are physically 'in the brain'; but this doesn't explain why someone develops anxiety in the first place, and nor does it explain the reason behind an individual's specific 'anxiety' triggers.

One question it does throw up is, "**once the fear pathways have become overactive, does this 'overactivity' then become an additional and distinct problem; a problem that persists 'after' the anxiety triggers have been resolved**? Does this explain the situation in which people are left with an overactive fear system even though there is no longer any fear *stimulus* or trigger? It also throws up the question of whether it is possible for their brain structures to return to normal levels of activity with no more false alarms.

This idea is fairly well developed in what is called the 'neuromatrix theory',[12] which I first came across when I was studying for my master's degree in pain medicine.

One of the main aims of trying to understand the *mechanisms* that are going on in the brain when someone has anxiety disorder is to then investigate if there is anything about those *mechanisms* that can be exploited in terms of treatment.

Let's take a look at how this works. First, here is an over-simplification of anxiety and panic disorder:

Stimuli + Altered Brain Physiology = Anxiety and Panic Disorder.

(Yes, I know, really quite simple)

Treatments, therefore, can be targeted at the ***Stimuli*** or at the ***Altered Brain Physiology***, or ***both***.

Changing the Stimuli

First, let's look at the stimuli, or trigger. Obviously, one of the ways we try to manage anxiety is to avoid the 'triggers'. For some people the trigger is public speaking, and so if that person can avoid public speaking, then they can avoid anxiety. For other people, however, certain thoughts or everyday environments can trigger anxiety.

In this case, anxiety 'triggers' are not so easy to avoid, and trying to avoid them can lead to a greatly reduced quality of life.

And just in case you hadn't noticed, staying at home, not socializing, and avoiding friends and

family doesn't equate with a delightful and flourishing life.

The variability of the trigger, therefore, is a major determinant of the impact that anxiety can have on a person's life, and long-term avoidance of the trigger may not be feasible or successful. Learning to cope with the anxiety in the presence of the trigger is therefore another common treatment approach, and this may be achieved with cognitive behavioural therapy (CBT).

CBT is also used to identify incorrect or false thoughts and then uses *questioning* and *reasoning* to challenge these thoughts in order to diffuse their effects. This is referred to as cognitive restructuring and is based on logic and evidence. CBT uses a range of approaches to reduce or squash the various 'thought viruses' that trigger panic attacks and anxiety, and it is tailored to the individual – well that's the theory anyway.

Working through personal issues with counselling or some other version of psychotherapy is another approach. Hypnosis comes to mind. Neurolinguistic programming is another. In fact, there is a plethora of programs, alternative treatments, techniques, spiritual practices and the requisite 'hocus pocus' that people use to try and change the trigger.

And fair enough too – if you had anxiety disorder you'd probably consider trying everything.

For me, I couldn't touch any of the treatments or ideas that smelt in the slightest like bull&^%$.

Remember that I had a problem with *uncertainty* and I had a problem with *false beliefs and false hope*. The thought that I might go to a practitioner who gave me a *reason* and *treatment* for my anxiety that took me down a dead end wild goose chase and added baggage to my already overloaded mind was just too much.

This is the same problem that many people with chronic pain have. They go from practitioner to practitioner, and from one healing modality to another, always seeking a cure, but picking up a deluge of rubbish along the way that forever integrates with their beliefs about their pain, and very often acts as an obstacle to their recovery.

I know this is the case from the research literature on chronic pain, and also from the hundreds and hundreds of patients I have consulted who have chronic pain and who have picked up various concepts and explanations along the way – concepts and explanations that have been refuted by research.

Anyway, again I digress; but if you are interested in my perspective on pain, I've written a brief introductory book on the topic called, *The Pain Experience: Navigating the Network*.

This book is available at www.thepainexperience.com

I've also written a basic introduction to the uncertainties of medical diagnosis in my book, So, *what's wrong with me?: Understanding the uncertainties of medical diagnosis*.

This book is available at www.niclucas.com/books

In summary, for any of the psychological therapies that are aimed at changing the *triggers of anxiety* to work, they have to impact the overactive fear pathways and modify our brain physiology; but the focus of the treatment is primarily on the trigger, and not the brain physiology. Evidence for effectiveness of these approaches is presented in chapter 5.

Changing the Brain

Using pharmacotherapy (code for drugs) to modify or reduce the over activity in fear pathways is the obvious bio-medical approach. It would be easy to reproduce a list of medications here, however I have resisted this temptation. If you want technical information on the drugs and how they work, follow this link.

Instead of details, I'm going to introduce the drugs *conceptually*.

Imagine a ball. This ball is going to represent a group of neurons in the amygdala – that server in your brain that is associated with an overactive anxiety response.

Imagine that you are bouncing the ball.

Now imagine that the ball is filling up with more and more air and has more pressure in it, and now it's bouncing faster, faster, and even faster.

Imagine it completely full of pressure – no room for any more air. Hear how it 'pings' off the ground.

Now imagine it bouncing so fast that your hand can't keep up with it.

You have just imaged *overactivity.*

Now, imagine that ball slowing down and becoming still.

The air is escaping and the ball is becoming flat.

You try to bounce it…but we all now how unsatisfying it is to try and bounce a flat ball.

You have just imaged *underactivity.*

Now imagine millions of different coloured balls, all with different amounts of pressure and different rates of bouncing. The balls represent the nerves, and the colours represent the different types of nerves; the pressure represents how *able* they are to bounce, and the rate of bouncing represents just how often these nerve cells are firing and releasing chemicals.

This is what is going on in the different deep brain servers that are involved in producing ***emotion***. There are many things that can impact how much pressure is in each ball and how fast each is bouncing. The various drugs prescribed for anxiety modify one or more of these things, by either decreasing or increasing the rate of bouncing or the pressure in the balls.

What is important to understand, however, is that we can't presume that the drugs return things to 'normal'. In fact, there's nothing *normal* about your brain physiology being altered by the presence of an external agent.

Drugs are like 'software' installed onto the server to change how it functions – but sometimes the software isn't a great match, doesn't share the same operating system, and just doesn't work that well. It can also interfere with how other 'host' software programs are running, and cause these to do weird things.

Your IT department asks your consciousness, "did you install any third party software, because our IT support doesn't offer support for these programs. We only look after host (our own) software".

My point here is that drugs *do* modify our brain physiology and they *may* induce an emotional experience that resembles *normality*, and this *may* just do the trick and resolve anxiety.

Medication, while it may reduce anxious or panicky feelings, may also induce other emotions or physical symptoms that aren't welcome. It may interfere with other emotions that we didn't have a problem with before. In addition, withdrawal of these drugs may leave the operating system in havoc.

Summary

The main take home message is that anxiety and panic are associated with dysfunction of the brain circuits that regulate fear. Panic is thought to start in an abnormally sensitive fear network, cantered in the amygdala. The amygdala itself is linked to breathing centres, heart centres, gut centres, bladder and bowel centres, and stress response centres.

This is why so many different body systems are associated with anxiety and panic. Sensations such as nausea or palpitations may act as a trigger, or they may be symptoms of anxiety and panic such a rapid heartbeat, perspiration, or difficulty breathing.

There are really only main two strategies to help overcome anxiety. You either deal with the triggers, or you directly modify the brain physiology. Of course, for each of these strategies there are a multitude of options. Each of these strategies has a reason for *why* it should work, but the most important questions are *does* it work, and *will* it work for you? I tackle this question in the next chapter.

Biological Findings	Panic Disorder	Generalised Anxiety Disorder	Social Anxiety Disorder	Obsessive Compulsive Disorder	Posttraumatic Stress Disorder
Hyperactive locus coeruleus	•	•	•		
Dysregulated serotonergic system	•	•	•	•	•
Decreased GABA-BZD receptor binding complex	•	•	•		
Hypersensitive brain stem $C0_2$ receptors	•				
Hypersensitive fear network	•	•	•		•
Genetic component	•	•		•	
Decreased dopamine			•	•	
Hyperactive orbitofrontal-limbic-basal ganglia circiuitry				•	
Autoimmune response in some people				•	
HPA axis dysregulation					•
Dysregulated opioid system					•
Hippocampal toxicity					•
Neuropeptide Abnoramilties				•	

Table 1: Neurological dysfunction associated with anxiety disorders

5

Make it go away: A look at treatment and management

In this chapter, I'm not going to go into the details of *how* these treatments might work[5] – for how they work is slightly irrelevant. The most important question is, "do they work"? Many people don't even ask this question, they just *expect* that the things that are called 'treatments' are, actually, treatments; meaning that they *work*.

In my experience in health care and research over the last 15 years, I can confidently say that many things that are called 'treatments' are nothing of the sort – because ***they don't work***. There may be all sorts of complicated and scientific sounding theories for *how* or *why* they should work…but when they are actually tested to see if they *do* work, the answer comes back negative – they don't work any better than a pretend treatment. This is true for some medications, some surgical procedures, some psychological therapies, and some alternative therapies.

So, if you really want to know if a treatment works, you need to test it to see if it *does work*. Testing the treatment usually involves some form of controlled clinical trial, in which the treatment is compared to a control group, which

5 For a detailed description of drug action, visit www.pdrhealth.com/drugs/rx/rx-a-z.aspx

might use a pretend treatment, some other form of treatment, or a 'do nothing but wait and see' option.

And the control group is what is missing from the typical marketing campaigns of anxiety treatments. The promoter says, "hey, this worked for me and I've got these testimonials from other people saying it worked for them". But what is missing is the other data – the number of people who tried it and found that *it didn't work for them*.

There's nothing the matter with testimonials – they can really help someone make the decision to try a certain technique or treatment. It's always better to know that some people have tried it and found it useful.

All I'm saying is that testimonials aren't proof enough that a treatment really works – even though testimonials are part of the picture. Even those treatments that have been shown to work scientifically, often work 'better' because *other* people have confidence in them.

Before we go any further, I should define what I mean by "works". What does it mean when we say that a treatment "works"? We want to know the outcome. Exactly 'what' does the drug achieve in terms of improving the situation? Exactly 'what' will happen if I spend $2,000 on psychotherapy?

In terms of anxiety and panic disorder, I consider the term "works" to mean that the treatment improves psychological symptoms, improves interpersonal functioning, improves

social functioning, and improves quality of life.

And further, it is not enough to 'improve' these things a little bit – I want them to be improved a **big bit**.

Sometimes, even a little improvement can be a huge relief, but for a treatment to *work* it means that people can enjoy life without anxiety intruding upon their day-to-day activities and without destroying their hope for the future.

But we're not done yet, because the way I see it, "works" also means that side effects are absent or negligible. So, for any treatment that "works" we also have to ask, "but are there any side-effects"? Why is this important? Take the following example.

"Yes, doc, thanks for the script…ummmm…do these drugs actually work".

"Yes" says the doc, "they'll help reduce your anxiety and get you a bit of sleep".

This is code for, "Yes, you will have a reduction in your feelings of anxiety – in fact you may have a reduction in your *feelings*. You may feel numb and lack the ability to experience any emotion – including joy, excitement, and hope. Oh…and the drug makes you quite drowsy, so you'll be tired most of the day. Yes, that's about it. You'll feel emotionally numb and tired all day long. But you wont feel anxious. So, you see, the drug *does* work".

"OK, ummm, right…and are there any side effects I should know about"

"All drugs can have side-effects" says the doc. "Show me a drug without side effects and I'll show you an ineffective drug. Read the documentation or speak to the pharmacist and get back to me if you have any questions."

This is code for, "damn right there are side-effects... there are so many that I really don't have the time to go through them all with you, and then answer all the questions you should reasonably have; especially the question about how the drug I'm recommending to treat your anxiety might actually *cause* you to have more anxiety".

Now, **I've given a fairly pessimistic example here**, and I have to 'fess up...this was my experience, and so I've given a biased account. There are, of course, excellent doctors who do have an interest in providing excellence in mental health care. I justify this biased representation by saying that **you** are the one with anxiety and **you** are the one who is at risk of being given inappropriate or ineffective treatment, and **you** are entitled to know what treatment **you** are being prescribed, what **you** can expect it to achieve for **you**, and what risks are involved for **you**.

It is the consumer advocate coming out in me.

In this introductory section, I've unpacked what it means when we say a treatment "works", including the fact that it should work very well, and it shouldn't have side effects that are as bad or worse than the anxiety or panic.

Now let me take you through the various treatments for which I have been able to find scientific studies – there are quite a few. I've broken the treatments down into sections based on the species of practitioner that is most likely to recommend them. I've chosen somewhat cynical headings for these practitioners – because, well, it's my book and I can. It's meant to make all of this serious stuff a little light-hearted, and if I offend anyone please feel free to leave a comment on my blog at www.niclucas.com

Oh, and one other major point. There are different types of anxiety disorder. Some of the evidence cited below relates to generalized anxiety disorder, whereas other evidence relates to social anxiety disorder, or panic disorder. I have pointed this out where necessary, and at the end of the chapter I have included a table that summarises the available evidence.

Lastly, this chapter is not meant to provide comprehensive information on the specific treatments for specific individuals – it's a general knowledge chapter. In order for you to fully understand which treatment is best for you – especially when it comes to medication or formal psychological therapy – you need to consult with an appropriately qualified, and hopefully very nice and understanding practitioner.

Drug Dealers

General medical practitioners (family physicians) and psychiatrists are the licensed drug dealers in our society. Whilst not all of them offer drugs for the treatment of anxiety and panic disorder…very many do. Drugs are the biomedical treatment of choice and their purpose is to alter the 'brain physiology' part of that oversimplified anxiety equation I mentioned earlier:

Stimuli + Altered Brain Physiology = Anxiety or Panic Disorder

The approach I've decided to take is to discuss the class of drug and whether or not it has been found to be effective. First, however, I'll introduce this section by referring to a review paper published in 2005 by Baldwin and Polkinghorn.[13]

They evaluated all of the available evidence on various drugs in order to answer the questions: (1) What is the most effective first-line treatment for generalised anxiety disorder; and (2) What is the best intervention if someone doesn't respond to the first line treatment.

After reading pages and pages of details, and referring to annoyingly large tables of statistics, I eventually came to the answers.

First, it would seem that selective serotonin reuptake inhibitors (SSRI), such as fluoxetine (Prosac), citalopram (Celexa), and sertraline (Zoloft) are *probably* the best drugs of choice for first-line treatment…let me repeat that…

…*probably* the best drugs of choice.

And if they don't work, maybe *try* venlafaxine (Effexor)…

The best that science can throw up gets pre-empted with the words *probably* and *try*.

I'd like some more convincing prose, wouldn't you?

Anyway, let's take a closer look at the evidence for each specific drug class.

Selective Serotonin Re-uptake Inhibitors (SSRI's)

In the review mentioned above by Baldwin and Polkinghorn[13] it is reported that, esclitalopram, paroxetine, and sertraline have scientific evidence of their effectiveness. Dhillon and colleagues[14] reviewed the literature on escitalopram, which was found to reduce the symptoms of anxiety and panic disorder irrespective of age, gender, chronicity, weight and concurrent depressive disorders. In the treatment of those with panic attacks, about 50% had no attacks during the treatment; but get this, 38% of those who took the placebo drug had no attacks either.

So while 50% of those taking the 'real' drug had no attacks, 38% taking the 'pretend' drug were also panic-free. You know, these pretend drugs are pretty good aren't they…?

Some may argue that placebo's are OK to use. They'll say that, "It's fine to give a medication to a patient – so long as it works, right?" Well, not necessarily and this is a complicated and controversial issue. I can't get into it here; suffice to say that it's not really OK to give someone a drug that has potential side effects, if that drug isn't anymore effective than a pretend drug.

Overall it would seem that SSRI's *are* the best drugs to try for the first line treatment of anxiety or panic disorder – assuming of course that drugs are going to be your first line treatment choice.

But what about the side effects…remember those?

The side effects of SSRI's can be grouped into physical symptoms like aches pains and rashes, sexual symptoms such as loss of sexual interest, performance problems, and reduced satisfaction, and then there are the blood clotting problems, especially if being taken in conjunction with non-steroidal anti inflammatory drugs (such as ibuprofen).

The other concerning side effect of SSRI's is the doubling of suicidal thoughts in adults and children, from 1-2% to 2-4%, and an increase in suicide attempts.[15]

Clearly, SSRI's can be helpful…but their side effects may be too much for people to use in the long, or even short term. These drugs are not lollies. They're not harmless. So if you're currently taking them, or are thinking of taking them, then make sure that you discuss the potential side effects with your doctor.

What other drugs are you likely to come across in your campaign to overcome anxiety or panic disorder?

Say 'hello' to the BZD's.

Benzodiazapines (BZDs)

For many years BZD's were the physician's treatment of choice for anxiety – the first line treatment. In 2007, Martin and colleagues[16] published the most rigorous scientific evaluation of BZD's for the treatment of generalised anxiety disorder (GAD). In the introduction of their paper they outline that BZD's are known to be ineffective in 25-30% of people with GAD.

The BZD's are also known to generate a high level of physical and psychiatric dependency. In addition, BZD's are known to produce sedation, reduced coordination, cognitive impairments, and increased accident proneness. So, summarising the BZD option. They might help. They might produce bad side effects. And you might become addicted.

OK, now that's established, let's look at the evidence for whether they do, actually, work.

Martin and colleagues[16] searched far and wide for any and all research on these drugs in the treatment of GAD. They found 1,217 articles, but after closer inspection, only

137 were relevant. Left with only 137, they then critiqued each article to see if it was any good, and whether or not it answered the question about whether BZD's actually work.

Of the 137 articles, 113 had to be ditched for various reasons...many because they were just bad science. Now that they were left with the 23 articles that were actually any good, they could go about looking at what each study found and what it all meant, collectively. In the discussion, they state:

"This systematic review failed to find convincing evidence of the short-term effectiveness of benzodiazepines in the treatment of generalised anxiety disorder."

"Benzodiazepines do not even prove to be definitively superior to placebo in the short term".

For impact, read those conclusions again and let them sink in. A class of drugs that were for many years the first line treatment provided to millions of people with anxiety have been found in numerous clinical trials to be no more effective than pretend drugs (placebos). In order to provide some insight into the complex world of medical research, I'll take you through another 'review' published two years earlier by Kapalan and DuPont.[17] These authors published a paper that claimed to review the effectiveness of BZD's, and also looked at safety issues such as side effects, tolerance, dependence and withdrawal.

Unlike Martin and colleagues, Kapalan and DuPont do not tell us how they found the scientific articles they used, how many articles they used, how they chose the ones they included in their review, or how they ranked them for quality. Interestingly, they concluded:

"Benzodiazepines have demonstrated efficacy in treating patients with anxiety disorders… Benzodiazapines **remain the mainstay in the treatment of anxiety**."

Now this is a clearly different conclusion to that of the more recent and rigorous review by Martin and colleagues!

Even more interesting is the fact that a pharmaceutical company funded the review by Kapalan and DuPont. Now it would be easy to be cynical and conclude that Kapalan and DuPont presented a biased viewpoint – but let's give them the benefit of the doubt. The reality is that this whole medical research thing is highly complex; and if the medical specialists are disagreeing about how useful a certain drug is, then there's not much chance that a general medical practitioner working in 'the trenches' is going to be any better informed.

My take on this is that the more recent work of Martin and colleagues[16] provides a more rigorous account of BZD's in the treatment of anxiety. Their answer to the question of whether BZD's work is that there is *no evidence that they work any better than a placebo* – but that they come with the *potential for dependency and unwanted side effects.*

This view is also shared by the American Psychiatric Association whose main instruction manual for psychiatrists lists SSRI's as the first line treatment for anxiety disorder, not BZD's.[18]

Antidepressants

Antidepressants are called antidepressants because they were found to help some people with depression – **clever huh**. This doesn't mean, however, that the only effect they have is on depression. In fact, at different doses, antidepressants are used in certain conditions for pain relief. Antidepressants have also been found to be helpful in some people with anxiety; not because these people are depressed, but because antidepressants help quieten down the *anxiety system*.

One minor thing to point out about antidepressants is that some of them are SSRI's, which have already made an appearance above. This can make things a little confusing, because certain drugs are classed in different ways.

In 2003, Kapczinski and colleagues[19] produced one of the most comprehensive review papers on the use of antidepressants to treat generalised anxiety disorder. Like Martin and colleagues did for BZD's, Kapczinski searched for every available research study ever performed on the use of antidepressants for anxiety, weeded out the bad science, and then looked at what the remaining good science had to say.

Antidepressants like imipramine (Tofranil), venlafaxine (Effexor) and paroxetine (Paxil) were found to be better than placebo drugs for anxiety, however they only worked in 1 out of every 5 patients. Re-worded for impact, antidepressants don't work in 4 out of every 5 people with anxiety that leave the doctors office with a script.

Curamba...that's only a 20% hit rate!

Kapczinski[19] concluded that there is evidence that antidepressants are better than placebo's in treating generalized anxiety disorder, but that further studies were needed to find out which antidepressants should be used for which patients, because different drugs modify *different* symptoms of anxiety.

Do you get this? You take an antidepressant for anxiety – you hope it that you're the 1 out of 5 that it *works* for – but even if it does *work* it may only be for *certain* symptoms.

And of course, there are the usual tag along suspects: **nausea, dry mouth, insomnia, constipation, drowsiness, anorexia, sexual dysfunction and flatulence** – and of course these don't just happen in isolation – they can occur together. Imagine having to explain yourself when your doctor asks if you're feeling better:

"Well Doc...I guess I'm not feeling as anxious...but I can't sleep even though I'm tired all the time. I'm not hungry and don't enjoy my favourite foods. I can't kiss because I've got a dry mouth. I'm constipated and I've got flatulence, which probably also explains why I've got sexual dysfunction. But overall, I guess I am feeling less anxious"

Of particular importance is that these findings were supported in a review published a year later by Schmitt and colleagues,[20] which means that different experts from different parts of the world agree about the effectiveness and side effects of antidepressants for anxiety, which is quite a **feat** really.

And get this; there is even a systematic review[21] of all the clinical trials for treatment of ***anti-depressant induced sexual dysfunction***! So, basically, they're trying to figure out the best drug to give people who have sexual dysfunction that is *caused* by antidepressants.

In 2008, Hansen and colleagues[22] produced a report on the second generation antidepressants for the treatment of social anxiety disorder. After reviewing all of the available evidence they conclude that antidepressants are effective in social anxiety disorder, and that there is no difference in the effectiveness of escitalopram, fluvoxamine, paroxetine, sertraline, and venlafaxine.

But, be warned, the side effects produced by each drug *do* differ, and so you would need to have a serious talk with your doctor before you decide which antidepressant to take – if indeed you decide to take one.

Azapirones

Azapirones act like serotonin in the brain and have been used to treat generalised anxiety disorder. In 2006 Chessick and colleagues[23] report that clinical trials for these drugs have given *conflicting results* and that it is ***not really known if they are useful*** **as a first line treatment**.

Blimey. How many people are on these things?

Anyway, the review by Chessick[23] for azapirones was again the most comprehensive performed to date. They searched every scientific database, library, and conference proceeding for everything they could find on the topic.

Then they cut out the dross, kept what was worthwhile, ranked it according to a scientific quality scale and then summarised their findings. Out of 36 good quality studies they found that azapirones do seem to work better than pretend drugs (placebos), but were probably **less effective** than BZD's and were also **less tolerable** than BZD's – a set of characteristics that just doesn't look good on the CV. Remember, BZD's aren't that crash hot either…

In addition, none of the studies could answer the question about whether azapirones were better than antidepressants, psychotherapy, or a naturally occurring herbal remedy called kava kava…

GABA

This class of drugs are actually quite interesting – because there is this naturally occurring drug in the brain called GABA that is reduced in people with anxiety and panic disorder. Zwanzger[24] reports that one brain imaging study demonstrated a 22% reduction of GABA in a certain part of the brain in patients with panic disorder.

In true biomedical style, the pharmacists thought to themselves, "maybe by increasing the amount of GABA in the brain we can help reduce anxiety and panic".

This thinking is fair enough, but can be problematic. **First** a reduction in GABA in certain parts of the brain could be *caused* by the anxiety or panic disorder, and not the other way around. There may be stacks of people walking around with reduced levels of GABA but who have never had a day of anxiety or panic in their lives.

Second, GABA is touted as being the most important neurotransmitter in the brain for turning off nerves – and if it is so important and so widespread, then I can imagine that there will be side effects.

So, what's the story with these 'GABA' drugs then? Well, GABA hardly even makes a mention in the official treatment guidelines published by the American Psychiatric Association.[1] Zwangzger[24] is up-beat about his research on rats and other animals, but doesn't have any solid proof in humans that GABA works. There has to be much more research on GABA before it makes its mark in the treatment of anxiety and panic disorders.

Shrinks

Cognitive Behavioural Therapy (CBT)

CBT is one of the most common forms of psychological therapy used to help treat anxiety disorder. The basic characteristics of CBT can be broken down into ***cognitive*** aspects and ***behavioural*** aspects. The aim of the cognitive aspects of CBT is to identify irrational thoughts that provoke anxiety, and then to challenge these thoughts and underlying beliefs.

These cognitive approaches are then combined with behavioural tasks such as muscle relaxation and breathing techniques, keeping a diary, and specific skills training.

Remember the analogy I gave of the file transfer protocol – FTP – in which you upload new web pages to your server so that your server serves you up the new web page instead of the old one. Well, according to Wright and colleagues,[25] there are four major types of irrational thoughts that produce anxiety, and the aim of CBT is to identify these thoughts and change them – and CBT is the FTP program that you use.

The four major irrational thoughts to be modified are:

- Overestimation of the chance that a fearful event will happen.
- Exaggerated ideas about how severe the fearful event will be.
- Underestimation of their own coping abilities; and
- Underestimation of how much help other people can provide.

In terms of panic attacks, the emphasis is on helping the patient understand that **their estimates of impending doom are grossly exaggerated** and to help them change these beliefs or thoughts and teach them how to reduce their physical distress.[25]

Various techniques are used, but the common ones are: ***Socratic questioning***, which challenges people to think about what they are thinking about and generate alternative thoughts; ***visual imagery*** in which the person imagines a different and better outcome than what they are currently imagining; and ***examining the evidence*** about the truth or likelihood of their thoughts and fears.

CBT also includes ***relaxation training*** and ***breathing control*** in order to reduce the physiological agitation that is typical of panic attacks.

CBT also uses what is called ***graded exposure*** in which people are gradually exposed to the trigger of their anxiety, such as driving or public speaking, with the aim of increasing their tolerance to this trigger.

While it all sounds good in theory, I call this argument the "why it *should* work" argument. It's far more useful to know if CBT actually *does* work. In order to answer this question, Hunot and collegaues[26] systematically evaluated all of the available scientific studies on the effectiveness of CBT for anxiety disorder.

This review is the most comprehensive and rigorous of its type. The authors reviewed 85 studies and then discarded those that were irrelevant or poor quality, leaving only 23. Each of the studies used a CBT approach, and this was compared to either standard care, or some other type of psychological therapy.

Basically, people who received CBT were more likely to experience an immediate reduction in their anxiety compared to those people who received usual treatment. CBT was also found to be effective in reducing secondary symptoms such as depression. Unfortunately, none of the studies looked at the long-term benefits of CBT, and information about the side effects of psychological therapies was not reported.

It also wasn't clear if CBT was more effective than other psychological therapies, and more studies are needed before we know how effective CBT really is.

In 2005, Butler and colleauges[27] went for the 'big one'. They didn't just review individual clinical trials of CBT for anxiety disorder; they did a review of the reviews. They comment that CBT is one of the most extensively researched forms of psychotherapy, and found that CBT has a large effect in the treatment of social phobia, post-traumatic stress disorder, anxiety, and panic disorder with or without agoraphobia.

OK – that's not a bad wrap for CBT.

In 2007, Norton[28] and colleagues reviewed all of the relevant clinical trials to see if CBT was any better at treating one type of anxiety disorder over another. First, they found that CBT was effective in treating all types of anxiety disorders. Second, CBT appeared to be more effective for generalized anxiety and posttraumatic stress disorder than for social anxiety.

They also found, however, that while CBT was more effective than doing nothing, it wasn't better than relaxation treatment.

Hmmm…

In 2005 Wetherall[29] and colleagues looked at the effectiveness of CBT in the treatment of anxiety in later life, and found that relaxation training and CBT appeared to be effective for the subjective symptoms of anxiety and panic disorder. Their findings were reinforced three years later when in 2008, Hendriks and colleagues[30] reviewed 7 trials looking at CBT for the treatment of anxiety in people aged over 60.

Based on the collective evidence of these 7 trials they concluded that CBT was more effective than doing nothing and was a good alternative to antidepressants.

How do I translate all of this? Well, no one can get up on their soapbox and say with any authority that one psychological therapy is definitely better than another. It's all still up in the air and is probably different for different people.

Some people are advertising online that their system is the ***only*** system that works for anxiety. Some go as far as to say that psychotherapy doesn't work, and in fact makes anxiety symptoms *worse.*

The collective evidence from many controlled studies, however, authoritatively disputes these types of claims. In addition, a number of people *claim* that their programs are unique, when in fact they are not unique – and are classified as *psychotherapy.* One of the most popular online anxiety programs is totally based on CBT principles, yet claims in it's marketing material that psychological therapy doesn't work.

What can be said about CBT and relaxation training is that they are better than doing nothing, and they are a good alternative to antidepressants – all of which sounds good to me. Not everyone benefits however, so it's not like you can go and have some CBT and hey presto you're cured. I have met numerous people for whom CBT *didn't* seem to help at all. This anecdotal evidence confirms to me – again – that what works for some people, might not work for others.

It's also important to recognise that psychological therapy is also personality dependent. Basically, this means that if you don't *connect* with your therapist then your response wont be as good as it could be if you *did* connect with your therapist.

And there we go again as humans – complicating things!

Psychodynamic psychotherapy

The primary aim of psychodynamic psychotherapy is to delve into and reveal the conflicts of a person's unconscious mind in order to relieve angst or tension. It's a bit like psychoanalysis and also focuses on early childhood experiences, but it is designed to be quicker and less intensive.

Abbass and colleagues[31] reviewed all of the available literature on psychodynamic psychotherapy to find out if it actually works for mental disorders. In relation to anxiety, moderate effects were found in those who received therapy compared to those who didn't receive any treatment, but these effects didn't appear to last in the long term.

As with many areas of medicine and psychology, more studies are needed before any definitive statements can be made. And what this basically means is that we just don't know with any real certainty if these things work. It's a 'try and see' what happens approach, but 'trying' means spending both time and money on a particular therapy with no certainty that it's going to help.

And that's the unfortunate conundrum that you may be all too familiar with.

Combined Treatment: Pharmacotherapy and Psychotherapy (or drugs and shrinks)

OK, what about combining CBT with drug therapy – surely that's going to have a double-barrelled effect?

Three separate review papers have each tried to answer this question, and all three reviews were published in 2007; it must have been a hot topic that year…

Pull and colleagues[32] report that the combination of drug therapy and psychotherapy does *not* lead to better outcomes for anxiety compared to separate treatment with either one or the other treatment alone.

So basically, they report no clear benefit in combing these treatments.

This is really quite fascinating, because their report suggests that drug therapy is no better than psychotherapy, and that even combining the two doesn't give better results. So, one justifiable approach for the management of anxiety could be to go for psychotherapy and avoid the drugs– and their side effects.

Bandelow and colleagues[33] also completed a review of studies looking at combined treatment for anxiety disorder. They essentially agree with the review by Pull (described above); however Bandelow and colleagues report that for panic attacks, combined therapy was better than individual therapies alone.

Furukawa and colleagues[34] published a report looking at the combined use of CBT and drug therapy for the specific treatment of panic disorder with or without agoraphobia. Their results supported the findings of Pull and Bandelow; however for panic attacks, Furukawa report that combined therapy was effective in the early phase.

The take home message is that there is no stand out treatment. The drugs work in some people, but only help with certain anxiety symptoms, and may produce nasty side effects. Psychotherapy *does* have a large positive effect on anxiety disorders, however this effect is approximately the same as achieved with relaxation training.

Given the potential side effects of drugs, I see no compelling evidence that people should race out and get medication for their anxiety. I also see little justification for doctors to prescribe medication as a first line treatment for a new patient who turns up with anxiety – notwithstanding specific cases in which medication is essential to subdue the patient for safety reasons.

Of course, if the patient actually wants medication, then the doctor should take this into account.

I think that this is important information to know. If your health professional prescribes medication as the first treatment, you should question them on it. Why have they prescribed medication and not CBT, or relaxation? What evidence are they basing their decision on? Have they read the literature on this?

The view of the American Psychiatry Association is that there is evidence that drugs and CBT are on par for the short-term treatment of some anxiety disorders like social phobia or GAD, but that CBT reduces the risk of relapse. Some evidence indicates that CBT has good long-term effects in treating anxiety disorders.[18]

One of the main questions on people's minds is the cost of treatment. With regard to psychological therapy, people ask, "do I have to pay for therapy, or can I do it myself"?

Well, many people, myself included, *have* overcome anxiety and panic disorder without formal therapy, so it is possible.

I'm not making a recommendation for either approach. Some people reading this book may have already tried formal therapy; some people are too scared to try formal therapy; and still others wont go to see a health care professional about their anxiety disorder – preferring to keep it secret.

My personal experience is that there is definitely room for the non-formal treatment of anxiety and panic disorders, and this view is supported by a large systematic review by den Boer and colleagues[35] who state that the "**mental health care system does not have the resources to**

meet the extensive need for care of those with anxiety and depressive disorders".

In addition, Mayo-Wilson and Montgomery are planning a large systematic review on the effectiveness of what they call ***media delivered self-help therapy***, because so many people access self-help programs for anxiety and panic.[36]

Virtual Reality

The use of virtual reality technology allows health professionals to present challenging stimuli or triggers to their patients in the context of cognitive behavioural therapy, with a view to desensitising the patient to the stimuli.

Virtual reality exposure uses real-time computer graphics in combination with body tracking devices, visual displays, and other sensory input devices to present a participant with a computer generated virtual environment that changes naturally with movement. Studies have looked at using virtual reality for the treatment of the 'fear of flying', the 'fear of spiders' and panic disorder with agoraphobia.

In 2005, Pull[37] reviewed the relevant literature on virtual reality in the treatment of anxiety and mood disorders and reported that the technology was "promising". Their findings were limited because there was a lack of good quality clinical trials on which to make any firm conclusions. Later, in 2008, Powers and Emmelkamp[38] conducted another systematic review, and this time were able to find 13 relevant articles for review. These authors conclude that virtual reality exposure to the 'trigger' stimulus is effective in reducing symptoms.

My take on this is that virtual reality exposure may be beneficial in some people. The drawback is one of the limited availability of the technology. Not every one is going to be able to zoom out to their therapist for some virtual reality – well not yet anyway – but it is a promising treatment option.

Self-help and media-delivered treatments (like this book)

Because the availability of trained mental health care workers is limited and the demand for their services is high, there has **been a move to promote self-help approaches that are based on psychological treatments**. Bower and colleagues[39] searched for and reviewed all of the available literature on **self-help treatments** and found some evidence that they may be **more effective that usual care** in the short term.

Self-help treatments include what is referred to by the awkward name 'bibliotherapy', which just means treating the patient by giving them a book that includes education and strategies for reducing anxiety. 'Biblio' is Greek for book, so it just means book-therapy.

This book would be referred to as bibliotherapy – except that it is an electronic book. So, in order take into account of the many different mediums through which information is delivered these days, other researchers now prefer the term ***media-delivered treatment***. Anyway…this is all beside the point.

The point is to demonstrate that self-help programs are here to stay and these programs can be **as effective as**

those delivered by professionals.[35 40] The other important point is that people other than professionals *can* be involved in the delivery of programs aimed at helping people with anxiety.

For example, den Boer and colleagues[35] searched for all the research on the effectiveness of any kind of psychological treatment for anxiety disorders performed by what they called *paraprofessionals*. What they found was that paraprofessionals were more effective than usual care or pretend treatment, and were as effective as professionals.

For emphasis, "***as effective as professionals***".

So, what kind of species is a paraprofessional? Well, they're people who aren't professionals but who *assist* professionals...

Kaltenthaler[41] and colleagues conducted a systematic review of computerised cognitive behavioural therapy (CCBT); a self-help program that provides the potential benefits of cognitive behavioural therapy without needing to involve a therapist. They found 16 studies that ranged from poor to moderate quality. Five studies showed that computerised CBT was as good as actually attending a therapist; and four studies found CCBT to be ***more effective*** than usual treatment. The authors conclude that computerised CBT is potentially useful in the treatment of anxiety disorders and phobias.

Haven't computers and the Internet changed our lives? Now, for some people, self-help treatment provided over the Internet can be as effective as professional psychological therapy. This is great news, because many people will never attend formal therapy.

In 2007, Spek and colleagues[42] reviewed 12 randomised controlled trials specifically on internet-based cognitive behaviour therapy for symptoms of anxiety and depression. These authors conclude that Internet based CBT had a large effect, especially if combined with some therapist contact. These authors also found that computerised CBT had a larger effect on the symptoms of anxiety that those of depression.

So basically, computer based CBT programs look promising. Computers and the Internet provide a way of providing access to self-help materials like this book and the manual that goes with it. This is especially useful for people with mild symptoms who do not want to consult a GP or therapist. It is even more helpful for people who are housebound because of their anxiety – they can at least get some help over the Internet.

The sweaty Lycra crowd

Galen, a physician from the 2nd Century writes that,[43]

"the habit of the mind is impaired by faulty customs in food, drink and exercise . . . and these constitute the beginnings of severe diseases'.

There are also quotes and writings about the benefits of exercise from physicians in Greece, Turkey, Iran, China and Native America. So, physicians and thinkers centuries ago thought that exercise was important for mental health.

But we need more than quotes from ancient physicians.

Sometimes, one of the main arguments for *why* a particular healing system works is that it's been 'round for ages. Big deal I say. Just because an idea has been around for ages, doesn't mean that it is correct, true, or even close to the truth.

They thought the world was flat – for absolutely ages! They thought miasmas (bad air) caused cholera – for absolutely ages! People can be wrong for a long, long time...

Anyway, what's most important is that we now have a ton of direct evidence from scientific studies about the health benefits of exercise. In a systematic review looking at the effect that exercise has on mental health and well-being, Callaghan[43] reports that exercise improves cognitive functioning, reduces depression and, importantly for our purposes, *reduces anxiety.*

Callaghan[43] reports that multiple studies confirm that **exercise, especially aerobic exercise for more than 20 minutes, does help reduce the symptoms of anxiety, and is as effective as other interventions,** such as relaxation therapy (which if you remember, was as good as CBT). In another review,[44] it was concluded that the effect of exercise on psychological health was in some cases better than counselling alone.

This gist of this section is this: **go and do some exercise**. It's a no brainer. Just start doing some regular exercise. It wont necessarily be the whole answer – the total cure – but there are many reasons why you should exercise and virtually none that you shouldn't.

Some of the anxiety treatment products available online promote certain types of exercise. With respect, this is just their opinion and may simply be the type of exercise that worked for them. If someone is promoting Yoga as being the 'one' exercise you should do to get over anxiety, and you can't stand Yoga, then don't do it, and don't feel like you're missing out on the 'one true way'.

I didn't do Yoga, and I got over anxiety and panic disorder.

As an aside, when I first went to the doctor about anxiety, I wasn't given any advice about the beneficial effects of exercise or cognitive behavioural therapy? I wasn't given any literature on anxiety (bibliotherapy). I was told that therapy and counselling don't work and was given a prescription for benzodiazepines. Thanks Doc…but no thanks.

I did go to the psychiatrist for 'therapy', but he didn't talk to me about exercise or even general health – he preferred Zoloft (an SSRI) as a first line treatment.

Again, Thanks Doc…but no thanks. (Although I did carry the BZD's and the free pack of Zoloft around in my bag for 4 years – just in case.)

So, what else is there besides the conventional approaches? What are the alternatives?

The 'alternative' crowd …

Herbal Medicine

There are a surprisingly large number of herbal remedies available for anxiety that *supposedly* work. Well, while they supposedly work, the million-dollar question is, *"do they work"*? In order to answer this question, Jerome Sarris from the Department of Psychiatry at the University of Queensland looked at all of the relevant research on herbal remedies in the treatment of mental disorders, including anxiety.[2]

Across all the research studies, ***kava kava*** was the most extensively investigated herb, and Sarris concludes that substantial high-quality evidence exists for the use of kava in the treatment of anxiety. He also cautions that at present there is insufficient evidence for the use of many other herbal medicines in the treatment of anxiety disorders.

So, even though you may be loaded up with hundreds of dollars worth of herbal remedies from your health care practitioner – or friendly teenage shop assistant at the pharmacist(!) – and even though they've got lot's of books and theories about *why* these herbs should work – the fact is that they don't have enough good quality evidence that they *do*, in fact, *work*.

This doesn't mean you shouldn't necessarily try them – but as with all treatments, you should go in with your 'eyes open' – and given that herbs can interfere with other medications you may be taking, you should make sure that your herbalist knows which other drugs you are taking. It's also wise to run the idea of taking herbs past your doctor.

Examples of other herbs you may be prescribed or may find in the pharmacy are: **St John's Wort**; **Passion flower**; **Scullcap**; **Lemon Balm**; **Lemon Grass**; **California Poppy**; **Hawthorn Berry**; **Kampo formulations**; **Ashwagandha**; **Sour date seed**; **Brahmi**; and **Maidenhair**.

Given that Sarris did not find sufficient evidence for the majority of these herbs, I'll just provide a bit of a run down on what I've found out about the more common ones.

Kava Kava

Kava kava is a herbal preparation used in the treatment of anxiety disorders. For those who have ever visited the South Pacific Islands, it's also used as a traditional social and recreational drink that produces sedation.

Kava has been found to be effective in the treatment of anxiety, however it was withdrawn from the market in Switzerland and Germany due to cases of liver failure: a reminder that herbal remedies have side effects too and that just because it's 'natural' doesn't mean it's 'safe' – a common misnomer.

In 2005, Witte and colleagues[46] conducted a systematic review of research studies to investigate whether or not a kava **extract** was effective in the treatment of non-psychotic anxiety disorders. While there is a need for more studies, they report that the kava extract (WS®1490) is effective in the treatment of anxiety disorders and is an alternative to benzodiazepines, selective serotonin re-uptake inhibitors (SSRIs) and other antidepressants.

Sarris[2] reports that both anxiety and depression were reduced when *kava* was used in the treatment of anxiety in perimenopausal women. Both Witte and Stevinson[47] report that when used in isolation and in appropriate doses kava may be effective and well tolerated.

St John's Wort

St John's Wort is a herbal remedy used primarily for the treatment of moderate depression, and has been shown to be better than placebo and as effective as trycyclic antidepressants. Since antidepressants have been shown to have some benefit in the treatment of anxiety disorder, it would seem to make sense that St John's Wort might also have some effect on anxiety.

There has been very little research in this area, however one clinical trial[48] compared a combination of St John's Wort and Valerian with diazepam (a BZD), and was found to have some benefit.

The fact that St John's Wort is a herbal remedy does not mean that it is without side-effects. In 2003, Hammerness and colleagues[49] systematically reviewed all of the available research on the side effects of St John's Wort and report that the most common side effects are **skin reactions**, **fatigue**, **dizziness** and **headache**, **gastrointestinal symptoms** and a **dry mouth**, and get this, anxiety.

Hmmm...so you take St John's Wort for anxiety, and you're still feeling anxious, but now you don't know if this anxiety is due to 'your amygdala' or St John's Wort – and that could be a tricky situation to be in.

The good news, however, is that these side effects do seem to be rare – but it is always important to remember that drugs have side effects, whether they are 'pharmaceutical' or 'herbal'.

Valerian

Valerian is most commonly used to treat insomnia, however it has also been recommended as a treatment for anxiety. Miyasaka and colleagues[50] searched for all of the studies on valerian and found only one clinical trial, which compared valerian with diazepam (BZD) and a placebo.

It was only a small study, with 36 people, and the results were not surprising. There is no stand out amazing pill you can take that works for everybody with anxiety. In this study there was no difference between valerian and placebo – so the pretend 'drug' had the same effect as the valerian.

In addition, there was no difference between valerian and diazepam, which means that diazepam was about as good as a pretend drug – amazing stuff!

Valerian = diazepam = pretend drug → I wonder if anyone has patented the *pretend drug*?

Despite my facetious comments, more studies with more patients are needed before anyone can make any authoritative comments about valerian as a treatment option for anxiety disorders.

Yoga

The practice of yoga has become widespread, and it is generally presumed that yoga is associated with positive health effects. There is very little research, however, to support these claims. In 2005, Kirkwood and colleagues[51] reported their investigation into the effectiveness of yoga for the treatment of anxiety, and found that in general, the quality of the research studies was poor.

Basically, this means that it is not possible to make any authoritative claims about the effectiveness of yoga in the treatment of anxiety and there is a need for better studies.

As I discussed earlier, doing some exercise is a good idea – and if Yoga is your thing, then go do it.

Meditation

The practice of meditation is used widely for general health and well being, as well as for spiritual and religious reasons. Meditation is included in many programs of anxiety management, and is often included in the *behavioural* part of CBT. Meditation was for a long time associated with religious practices, however in 1976 Herbert Benson, a Harvard professor, wrote a book called ***The Relaxation Response*** in which he described his research into the effects of simple meditation.

He and his research group had discovered that a simple and non-religious practice of meditation achieved the same effects as those whose practice of meditation was linked to their spiritual or religious beliefs. Often associated with meditation is a procedure called ***progressive muscle relaxation*** during which the person sequentially contracts and relaxes the major muscle groups of the body whilst focussing on breathing and keeping their mind clear.

There is no doubt that many people perceive great benefit by practicing meditation.

But, sticking with the theme of really knowing if meditation "works" I needed to look at the research; and despite meditation being widely accepted and practiced, there is very little research in people with anxiety or panic disorder.

In 2006, Krisanaprakornkit and colleagues[52] published a systematic review of all the clinical trials looking at meditation as a treatment for anxiety. They searched all the standard medical and health science databases; searched conference proceedings and book chapters; and also contacted the leaders of spiritual and religious organisations – they wanted to make sure they'd searched far and wide.

Despite such a deep and broad search they found only two suitable clinical trials – which isn't enough to make any firm conclusions. The upshot of their review was that transcendental meditation is comparable with other kinds of relaxation therapies at helping reduce anxiety.

So, meditation represents yet another way to try and induce relaxation and reduce anxiety

– but it's not a stand out treatment that will guarantee your recovery and is no doubt just a part of the full treatment picture.

Reiki and Therapeutic Touch

Reiki is a conceptual system of *energetic* healing in which practitioners believe they facilitate the flow of *universal energy* to the patient that results in self-healing. Essentially, the practitioner places their hands gently over the area to be treated – and that's pretty much it.

Surprisingly, the National Health Services Trust and The Prince of Wales Foundation for Integrated Health in the UK recommend this form of healing for the management of chronic diseases. As is common for many alternative health practices, this *recommendation* was not based on a rigorous review of the effectiveness of Reiki, and was based instead on anecdotal evidence, poor quality reports, and the acceptance of the energetic concept at face value.

In a systematic review of all studies that tested the effectiveness of Reiki, Lee[53] and colleagues from the School of Complementary Medicine, Peninsula School of Medicine, conclude that there is no evidence to support the use of Reiki for any medical condition, including anxiety. The authors comment that the majority of studies were of low quality or were too small to prove or disprove the effectiveness of Reiki.

Therapeutic touch is supposed to work on essentially the same idea as Reiki, except practitioners don't even touch the patient, but hover their hands 3-5 cm's over the surface of the skin. They move their hands over the patient and seek to balance the patient's energy field.

Therapeutic touch was developed by Dolores Krieger, a Professor of Nursing, and is practiced by professionals to reduce anxiety, reduce pain and increase wound healing. It is taught in over 70 countries, so you'd think that there would be a lot of proof that it works, right?

Wrong. There isn't any proof whatsoever – other than anecdotal stories. Robinson and colleagues[54] searched far and wide and did not find one clinical trial on the effects of therapeutic touch for the treatment of anxiety.

The take home message is that no one knows if Reiki or therapeutic touch is effective for treating anxiety.

Spirituality, religion and psychotherapy

OK – what a doozey this section could be. First, the term spirituality means many different things to many different people. In this context, ***spirituality*** refers to transcendent experiences or understandings of God or other forces in the Universe, whereas ***religion*** refers to an institutionalised system of beliefs, values and activities.[55]

When anxiety hits, it would seem patently obvious that a persons underlying belief system will be caught up in their anxiety – or at the very least it will effect their understanding of ***why*** they are anxious and ***how*** they should go about overcoming it.

While some people believe that we are spirits having a physical experience on this earth, others don't conceptualise humans as being spiritual at all. This difference in belief about the very essence of what it is to be human colours a magnitude of concepts about the purpose of life, the way to live life, and the expectations we have of life.

Given the fragile existence of many people who are suffering anxiety and panic disorder, it seems obvious to suggest that their concept of spirituality and religion should be considered as part of their management. This is one area, however, that you don't want to barge into carelessly.

In 2007 Smith[55] wrote a review of the scientific studies which looked at the effect of incorporating spirituality and religion in the provision of psychotherapy. They examined 31 clinical trials and concluded that ***spiritual*** approaches can be effective if people apply their own religious or spiritual beliefs to their mental health or well-being.

This might seem like proving the obvious, but sometimes the obvious is important to prove. Remember, it was

obvious to many people for many years that the world was ***flat***. Anyway, as with most anxiety interventions covered in this section, more research is needed before these findings become definitive.

The take home message is that if a person has a spiritual or religious belief system, it may be of additional benefit to them if their treatment is provided in the context of their belief system.

I might also add, however, that a person's belief system may, in fact, be partly ***causing*** their anxiety. This was certainly the case in my own anxiety and panic disorder. Unpacking, challenging or deconstructing a person's beliefs is a tricky business

The take home messages from this chapter...

Exercise has been shown to help reduce anxiety symptoms, so start some form of regular exercise – but don't worry too much about what form of exercise you try, so long as it's something you enjoy doing and is convenient.

Drugs have not been shown to be superior to CBT, and relaxation therapy has been shown to be as effective as CBT – so if you're not comfortable with the side effects of drugs, then try CBT or relaxation therapy.

If you do want to try medication, then you could consider kava kava or St John's Wort – but also remember that these herbal remedies can **have side effects as well.** Of all the 'official' drug types, **SSRI's seem to be the best first line drug** – but again, consider their effectiveness in comparison to CBT, relaxation and exercise.

Using the **Internet** and books as a resource for CBT has also been shown to be useful, and if you can find anyone who uses virtual reality to manage phobias, then give that a try.

As for **energy healing**, like Reiki...well there's **no scientific evidence that it works.** But if this form of healing is consistent with your belief system, then **perhaps you should give it a try.**

All I would say is that you should also **consider using those treatments for which there *is* evidence of effectiveness.**

Lastly, always consider speaking with and being guided by a health professional experienced in dealing with anxiety disorders – someone who comes recommended if possible. This is especially so if you are really struggling and don't seem to be getting anywhere.

A final thought...

After reviewing the available evidence in my preparation for this book, I began to realise that there was room for me to describe a system for overcoming anxiety:

a system that was based on my own experiences and on the evidence from scientific studies and the principles of behavioural medicine.

The decision to write this book, and then the manual, was reinforced after reviewing a multitude of terrible websites about anxiety disorder and panic attacks. Ipser and colleagues[56] also reviewed the online anxiety websites – far more comprehensively than I did – and found that the majority were of only poor to moderate quality.

These findings were reported in the ***Current Psychiatry Reports***, which is an indication of how important Internet based self-help is becoming in academic circles.

Even though anxiety and panic disorder are common and severe, few people obtain professional treatment, and fewer still obtain specialty care. **The reality is that psychological therapies are often impractical due to the cost and time commitment, and many people prefer not to take medication.**

There needs to be an **effective and safe alternative** to help the people who are most likely to develop anxiety disorder and least likely to receive care.[35, 36]

So, I wrote a manual as a companion to this book, and called the manual, ***From Anxious to Happy: A manual for overcoming anxiety and panic attacks.***

This book and the manual are to be used together as a comprehensive resource, however they can be purchased and read separately.

In the manual, I describe a 7-step approach to overcoming anxiety and panic attacks. I describe every idea, concept and technique that I used to overcome anxiety and panic disorder, and I describe them in the chronological order in which I used them. The techniques I used toward the end of my disorder were different from the techniques I used in the middle, or at the very beginning – when I was 'freaked out'.

Each step I describe comes under the heading of one or more psychological therapies – but that's all academic and the 'label' of the technique isn't relevant. The manual is a practical guide to overcoming anxiety, and is based on everything I know and have experienced. If you would like more information or would like to download a copy, visit:

http://www.fromanxioustohappy.com

So, are you cured yet?

One of my favourite musicians, Ray Lamontagne, has a song titled, *Empty*. My favourite lyric in that song says,

"Well I looked my demons in the eye, laid bare my chest and said do your best to destroy me. Ya'see I've been to hell and back so many times I must admit you kind of bore me"

These lyrics sum up one of the key turning points in my recovery. I was bored. I was fed up. I had been to 'hell and back so many times' and I wasn't scared any longer. The first time was terrifying. And then I was terrified about going back again. The next visits were bad, but never as bad as the first visit.

Gradually, I began to realize that these panic attacks didn't really amount to much. I'd think, "oh, how boring, another one on it's way" and I'd just let it happen, knowing that it would pass and life would go on.

Once this had happened I was no longer scared of panic attacks. Of course, I didn't look forward to them, and I didn't enjoy them – they remained entirely unpleasant – but I was no longer scared. I was no longer having a *normal* anxiety response to this panic crap.

After reviewing the available evidence in my preparation for this book, I began to realise that there was room for me to describe a system for overcoming anxiety:

a system that was based on my own experiences and on the evidence from scientific studies and the principles of behavioural medicine.

I have documented all of the strategies and techniques that I discovered and used to overcome panic attacks and generalised anxiety disorder in a manual called *From Anxious to Happy: A manual for overcoming anxiety and panic attacks.*

The decision to write the manual was reinforced after reviewing a multitude of terrible websites about anxiety disorder and panic attacks. Ipser and colleagues[56] also reviewed the online anxiety websites – far more comprehensively than I did – and found that the majority were of only poor to moderate quality.

These findings were reported in the ***Current Psychiatry Reports***, which is an indication of how important Internet based self-help is becoming in academic circles. Even though anxiety and panic disorder are common and severe, few people obtain professional treatment, and fewer still obtain specialty care.

The reality is that psychological therapies are often impractical due to the cost and time commitment, and many people prefer not to take medication.

There needs to be an **effective and safe alternative** to help the people who are most likely to develop anxiety disorder and least likely to receive care.[35, 36]

I don't claim that the techniques in my manual are unique or the 'only way to recover from anxiety'. Each of the techniques, however, can be described as either cognitive therapy or behavioural therapy – although I never received any formal therapy or training in these methods – I just learnt them myself out of necessity.

By using my manual, you will be using a self-help approach – and there is evidence that self-help approaches are effective, for some people, in the treatment of anxiety disorders. It's important to remember, however, the there are different types of anxiety disorders and people have different levels of severity.

If you have anxiety or panic attacks, and you've never consulted a health professional, then you could start off with my manual – or one like mine, there are a few about. When it comes to anxiety, it probably pays *not* to over 'medicalize' it, and self-help strategies are a good first option.

In the manual, I describe a 7-step approach to overcoming anxiety and panic attacks. I describe every idea, concept and technique that I used to overcome anxiety and panic disorder, and I describe them in the chronological order in which I used them. The techniques I used toward the end of my disorder were different from the techniques I used in the middle, or at the very beginning – when I was 'freaked out'.

Each step I describe comes under the heading of one or more psychological therapies – but that's all academic and the 'label' of the technique isn't relevant. The manual is a practical guide to overcoming anxiety, and is based on everything I know and have experienced. If you would like more information or would like to download a copy, visit:

www.fromanxioustohappy/.com

My main concern is that you don't delay formal medical or psychological treatment if you really do need it. Neither you or I can officially diagnose your condition, and it may be important for you to seek general or specialist care, depending on your symptoms and the severity of them. If you feel as if you are going to harm yourself or someone else, then you should consult with your doctor as soon as possible – and make sure that you insist that they take you seriously.

If you have the luxury of choosing your own doctor or psychologist, then look for one with a special interest or additional qualifications in mental health. You want to go to a doctor who is interested in treating people with anxiety – the last thing you need to encounter in a health care practitioner is ambivalence.

I sincerely hope that this book has been of benefit to you and has helped you better understand anxiety and panic attacks.

List of resources mentioned in this book

http://www.anxiousbuthappy.com/definitions.html

www.fromanxioustohappy.com

http://www.pdrhealth.com/drugs/rx/rx-a-z.aspx

References

1 Diagnostic and Statistical Manual or Mental Disorders (DSM-IV Text Revision): 4th Ed. Edition. Washington DC: American Psychiatric Association

2 Sarris J. Herbal medicines in the treatment of psychiatric disorders: A systematic review. Phytotherapy Research 2007; 21: 703-716

3 Mirza I, Jenkins R. Risk factors, prevalence, and treatment of anxiety and depressive disorders in Pakistan: Systematic review. British Medical Journal 2004; 328: 794-797

4 Grigsby AB, Anderson RJ, Freedland KE, Clouse RE, Lustman PJ. Prevalence of anxiety in adults with diabetes a systematic review. Journal of Psychosomatic Research 2002; 53: 1053-1060

5 Deshmukh VM, Toelle BG, Usherwood T, O'Grady B, Jenkins CR. Anxiety, panic and adult asthma: A cognitive-behavioral perspective. Respiratory Medicine 2007; 101: 194-202

6 Dyrbye LN, Thomas MR, Shanafelt TD. Systematic review of depression, anxiety, and other indicators of psychological distress among U.S. and Canadian medical students. Academic Medicine 2006; 81: 354-373

7 Goldfarb MR, Trudel G, Boyer R, Pre?ville M. Marital relationship and psychological distress: Its correlates and treatments. Sexual and Relationship Therapy 2007; 22: 109-126

8 Davidson JRT, Connor KM, Swartz M. Mental illness in U.S. Presidents between 1776 and 1974: A review of

biographical sources. Journal of Nervous and Mental Disease 2006; 194: 47-51

9 Katerndahl D. Panic & plaques: Panic disorder & coronary artery disease in patients with chest pain. Journal of the American Board of Family Practice 2004; 17: 114-126

10 Carter R. Mapping the mind, 1998

11 Etkin A, Wager TD. Functional neuroimaging of anxiety: A meta-ana lysis of emotional processing in PTSD, social anxiety disorder, and specific phobia. American Journal of Psychiatry 2007; 164: 1476-1488

12 Melzack R. Evolution of the neuromatrix theory of pain. Pain Practice 2005; 5: 85-94

13 Baldwin DS, Polkinghorn C. Evidence-based pharmacotherapy of generalized anxiety disorder. International Journal of Neuropsychopharmacology 2005; 8: 293-302

14 Dhillon S, Scott LJ, Plosker GL. Escitalopram: A review of its use in the management of anxiety disorders. CNS Drugs 2006; 20: 763-790

15 Fergusson D, Doucette S, Glass KC, Shapiro S, Healy D, Hebert P, Hutton B. Association between suicide attempts and selective serotonin reuptake inhibitors: Systematic review of randomised controlled trials. British Medical Journal 2005; 330: 396-399

16 Martin JLR, Sainz-Pardo M, Furukawa TA, Martin-Sanchez E, Seoane T, Galan C. Review: Benzodiazepines in generalized anxiety disorder: Heterogeneity of outcomes based on a systematic review and meta-analysis of clinical trials. Journal of Psychopharmacology 2007; 21: 774-782

17 Kaplan EM, DuPont RL. Benzodiazepines and anxiety disorders: A review for the practicing physician. Current Medical Research and Opinion 2005; 21: 941-950
18 Hollander E, Simeon D. Anxiety Disorders. In: Hales RE, Yudofsky SC, Gabbard GO, eds. Textbook of Psychiatry: 5th Edition. Arlington, VA: American Psychiatric Publishing, Inc., 2008
19 Kapczinski F, Lima MS, Souza JS, Schmitt R. Antidepressants for generalized anxiety disorder. Cochrane Database Syst Rev 2003: CD003592
20 Schmitt R, Kratz Gazalle FK, Silva De Lima MS, Cunha A, Souza J, Kapczinski F. The efficacy of antidepressants for generalized anxiety disorder: A systematic review and meta-analysis. Revista Brasileira de Psiquiatria 2005; 27: 18-24
21 Taylor MJ, Rudkin L, Hawton K. Strategies for managing antidepressant-induced sexual dysfunction: systematic review of randomised controlled trials. J Affect Disord 2005; 88: 241-54
22 Hansen RA, Gaynes BN, Gartlehner G, Moore CG, Tiwari R, Lohr KN. Efficacy and tolerability of second-generation antidepressants in social anxiety disorder. International Clinical Psychopharmacology 2008; 23: 170-179
23 Chessick CA, Allen MH, Thase M, Batista Miralha da Cunha AB, Kapczinski FF, de Lima MS, dos Santos Souza JJ. Azapirones for generalized anxiety disorder. Cochrane Database Syst Rev 2006; 3: CD006115
24 Zwanzger P, Rupprecht R. Selective GABAergic treatment for panic? Investigations in experimental panic

induction and panic disorder. Journal of Psychiatry and Neuroscience 2005; 30: 167-175

25 Wright JH, Thase ME, Beck AT. Cognitive Therapy. In: Hales RE, Yudofsky SC, Gabbard GO, eds. Textbook of Psychiatry: 5th Edition. Arlington, VA: American Psychiatric Publishing, Inc., 2008

26 Hunot V, Churchill R, Teixeira V, Silva De Lima MS. Psychological therapies for generalised anxiety disorder. Cochrane Database of Systematic Reviews 2007; 2007: Art. No.: CD001848

27 Butler AC, Chapman JE, Forman EM, Beck AT. The empirical status of cognitive-behavioral therapy: A review of meta-analyses. Clinical Psychology Review 2006; 26: 17-31

28 Norton PJ, Price EC. A meta-analytic review of adult cognitive-behavioral treatment outcome across the anxiety disorders. Journal of Nervous and Mental Disease 2007; 195: 521-531

29 Wetherell JL, Sorrell JT, Thorp SR, Patterson TL. Psychological interventions for late-life anxiety: A review and early lessons from the CALM study. Journal of Geriatric Psychiatry and Neurology 2005; 18: 72-82

30 Hendriks GJ, Oude Voshaar RC, Keijsers GPJ, Hoogduin CAL, Van Balkom AJLM. Cognitive-behavioural therapy for late-life anxiety disorders: A systematic review and meta-analysis. Acta Psychiatrica Scandinavica 2008; 117: 403-411

31 Abbass AA, Hancock JT, Henderson J, Kisely S. Short-term psychodynamic psychotherapies for common mental disorders. Cochrane Database Syst Rev 2006: CD004687

32 Pull CB. Combined pharmacotherapy and cognitive-behavioural therapy for anxiety disorders. Current Opinion in Psychiatry 2007; 20: 30-35

33 Bandelow B, Seidler-Brandler U, Becker A, Wedekind D, Ru?ther E. Meta-analysis of randomized controlled comparisons of psychopharmacological and psychological treatments for anxiety disorders. World Journal of Biological Psychiatry 2007; 8: 175-187

34 Furukawa TA, Watanabe N, Churchill R. Combined psychotherapy plus antidepressants for panic disorder with or without agoraphobia. Cochrane Database Syst Rev 2007: CD004364

35 den Boer PC, Wiersma D, Russo S, van den Bosch RJ. Paraprofessionals for anxiety and depressive disorders. Cochrane Database Syst Rev 2005: CD004688

36 Mayo-Wilson E, Montgomery P. Media-delivered cognitive-behavioural and behavioural therapy (self-help) for anxiety disorders in adults. (Protocol). Cochrane Database of Systematic Reviews 2007; 2007: Art. No.: CD005330

37 Pull CB. Current status of virtual reality exposure therapy in anxiety disorders. Current Opinion in Psychiatry 2005; 18: 7-14

38 Powers MB, Emmelkamp PMG. Virtual reality exposure therapy for anxiety disorders: A meta-analysis. Journal of Anxiety Disorders 2008; 22: 561-569

39 Bower P, Richards D, Lovell K. The clinical and cost-effectiveness of self-help treatments for anxiety and depressive disorders in primary care: A systematic review. British Journal of General Practice 2001; 51: 838-845

40 Van Boeijen C, Boeke J, Van Oppen P, Blankenstein N, Cherpanath A, Van Dyck R, Van Balkom T. Efficacy of self-help manuals for anxiety disorders in primary care: A systematic review. Effect van zelfhulphandleidingen voor angststoornissen in de eerstelijnszorg 2006; 49: 182-186

41 Kaltenthaler E, Parry G, Beverley C. Computerized cognitive behaviour therapy: A systematic review. Behavioural and Cognitive Psychotherapy 2004; 32: 31-55

42 Spek V, Cuijpers P, Nykli?c?ek I, Riper H, Keyzer J, Pop V. Internet-based cognitive behaviour therapy for symptoms of depression and anxiety: A meta-analysis. Psychological Medicine 2007; 37: 319-328

43 Callaghan P. Exercise: A neglected intervention in mental health care? Journal of Psychiatric and Mental Health Nursing 2004; 11: 476-483

44 Weyerer S, Kupfer B. Physical exercise and psychological health. Sports Med 1994; 17: 108-16

45 D'Silva B. This sporting life. The Observer Magazine volume 29th September, 2002; 77-78

46 Witte S, Loew D, Gaus W. Meta-analysis of the efficacy of the acetonic kava-kava extract WSÆ1490 in patients with non-psychotic anxiety disorders. Phytotherapy Research 2005; 19: 183-188

47 Stevinson C, Huntley A, Ernst E. A systematic review of the safety of kava extract in the treatment of anxiety. Drug Safety 2002; 25: 251-261

48 Ernst E. Herbal remedies for depression and anxiety. Advances in Psychiatric Treatment 2007; 13: 312-316

49 Hammerness P, Basch E, Ulbricht C, Barrette EP, Foppa I, Basch S, Bent S, Boon H, Ernst E. St. John's wort: A systematic review of adverse effects and drug interactions for the consultation psychiatrist. Psychosomatics 2003; 44: 271-282

50 Miyasaka LS, Atallah AN, Soares BGO. Valerian for anxiety disorders. Cochrane Database of Systematic Reviews 2006

51 Kirkwood G, Rampes H, Tuffrey V, Richardson J, Pilkington K. Yoga for anxiety: A systematic review of the research evidence. British Journal of Sports Medicine 2005; 39: 884-891

52 Krisanaprakornkit T, Krisanaprakornkit W, Piyavhatkul N, Laopaiboon M. Meditation therapy for anxiety disorders. Cochrane Database Syst Rev 2006: CD004998

53 Lee MS, Pittler MH, Ernst E. Effects of reiki in clinical practice: A systematic review of randomised clinical trials. International Journal of Clinical Practice 2008; 62: 947-954

54 Robinson J, Biley FC, Dolk H. Therapeutic touch for anxiety disorders. Cochrane Database of Systematic Reviews 2006

55 Smith TB, Bartz J, Richards PS. Outcomes of religious and spiritual adaptations to psychotherapy: A meta-analytic review. Psychotherapy Research 2007; 17: 643-655

56 Ipser JC, Dewing S, Stein DJ. A systematic review of the quality of information on the treatment of anxiety disorders on the internet. Current Psychiatry Reports 2007; 9: 303-309

For more information, resources, and a video presentation, please go to:

http://FromAnxiousToHappy.com

You can also watch and listen to a short song written and recorded by the author (Nic Lucas) - it's actually kinda cool to hear a medical researcher play guitar and sing from the heart.

3185142R10076

Printed in Great Britain
by Amazon.co.uk, Ltd.,
Marston Gate.